LORD OF THE SWAMP

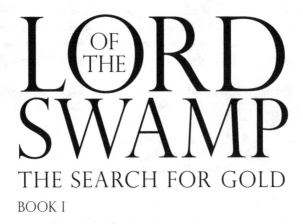

LORD OF THE SWAMP

THE SEARCH FOR GOLD

BOOK I

CALVIN RAY DAVIS

ARCHWAY
PUBLISHING

Archway Publishing books may be ordered through booksellers or by contacting:

Archway Publishing
1663 Liberty Drive
Bloomington, IN 47403
www.archwaypublishing.com
844-669-3957

ISBN: 978-1-6657-4927-5 (sc)
ISBN: 978-1-6657-4929-9 (hc)
ISBN: 978-1-6657-4928-2 (e)

Library of Congress Control Number: 2023916167

Print information available on the last page.

Archway Publishing rev. date: 09/12/2023

This novel is for all those who've been bullied in life; I've been in your shoes. Don't ever stop believing in yourself. Know that you are more than enough and never give up on your dreams.

ACKNOWLEDGMENTS

Thanks to my editor, Cynthia McCoy, of more than twenty years; you rock. To Julia Meadows, your help in this project is highly appreciated. To my fan reading club, Jimmy Davis, Janet Krull, Frank Amico, Karen Mulberry, Elaine Lyons, Na Baker, Jo Baker, Bonita, and Richard Harrison, thank you all for your time and feedback and making me love this story even more.

01

"I'm too young to die! I'm only a kid!" Tears stung my eyes.

I stood at the top of the stairs with my back to the door, looking down. The beam from the flashlight sent eerie glows over the room, leaving small sparkling streaks glistening on the dark waters below.

The water level was climbing the stairs rapidly. My rat terrier dog, Butch, stood next to me shivering and whimpering. He knew we were in serious trouble.

"Don't you give up on me!" Kyle's voice from the other side of the door was low. The tone in his voice frightened me.

I turned around and tried turning the doorknob. It wouldn't budge. It was as if it had been set in glue. I started twisting it back and forth, and then I pulled, yanked, kicked, and pushed on it. There was no opening it! My heart pounded in my chest.

"It won't open! *It won't open!*" I screamed above the rushing water that seemed to be crushing the wood of the houseboat. Its walls were closing in on me.

Water poured in everywhere. The sound of cracking glass from the old windows at the sides of the room was lost as the water rushed in. The bottom six steps were now below water, and the level was rising fast.

I cried out, "Kyle! Kyle, please get me out of here! I'm scared! I'm really scared!"

My heart slammed in my chest.

Would I drown?

I bent over and picked Butch up, and he looked into my eyes as if he knew it was the end of the road for both of us. He licked me on the cheek as the houseboat dropped three feet farther into the swamp.

Suddenly I was waist deep in water.

I dropped the flashlight and watched as it slid under the murky water sucking us down to our death.

"Kyle!"

02

"Ryan, could you stay after class for a moment? I would like to talk to you," Mrs. Phillips, my teacher, asked as the school bell rang.

I just nodded my head yes. There were things to do and places to go. I was twelve going on thirteen. I had a life, and it was the last day of school. Summer was waiting for me, and I was waiting for it.

I sat in class and watched as everyone left the room. Then it was just me and Mrs. Phillips. As teachers go, I had to admit she was kind of pretty, with her blonde hair pulled back behind her head, blue eyes behind cat-eyed glasses. The funky polka-dot blouse had to go though. It was downright ugly. Of course it matched her skirt that fell to the floor covering her feet.

"Could you come up here to my desk for a moment?" Her voice was so calm and nice. I had to admit she was one of the nicest teachers I had ever had. I couldn't help wondering how old she was.

"Yes, ma'am. Did I do something wrong?" I asked, wishing I were halfway to my house by now.

"Now, Ryan, you know you're one of the best students I have. I just wanted to talk to you for a minute."

"About what?" I swear the moment seemed to be frozen dead in its tracks.

"I wanted to talk about the short story you turned in for the final assignment. I've showed it to several other teachers in this school, and we're all beside ourselves that someone not even a teenager could write something this good. I wanted to tell you how proud I am to have you in this class. I've graded this test and would like you to enter this short story into a contest this summer. Would you be OK with that? But I must ask a question about this story."

"What about it?" I asked, wishing I were on my bike along the road back to my house. I really didn't hear all she'd just said to me.

"There is no need to take that sort of tone with me, young man."

"Yes, ma'am. I'm sorry."

"Did you write all of this?" she asked while tapping her finger on the desk. I could see she was tapping on the two-page story I had turned in.

"Yes, ma'am."

"Remind me again, how long have you been writing stories?"

"Since I was about five years old—almost a decade."

"Do you realize what year this is?"

"Yes, ma'am; it's 1977."

"You see, I've read this short story at least a dozen times, and I'll tell you, I am in awe of the purity of it. Are you sure you didn't get an adult to write this?"

"No, ma'am; I wrote every word of it."

"What about the contest? Would you like me to enter this story in it?"

"Sure."

I looked at the grade as she handed me the paper. I made an A plus. That was cool.

I said thank you as I handed it back to her. I would see her later in the summer since she lived right down the street from our house. She said to stop by her house in a couple of days, and she would give me the information on the contest.

"So what are you doing for the summer?" Mrs. Phillips asked.

"I turn thirteen next Friday."

"Happy birthday."

"Thank you. My older cousin, Kyle, is coming into town. I get to spend the entire summer with him."

"Well, do tell. That should be a great summer for you. I hope that you will write about it."

"Yes, ma'am, every single word. I hope you have a great summer."

"Thanks."

I found myself almost floating to the door. I had to get out. I had to make a run for it, to get away from school and get into my own imagination.

I walked to the door, and it took all my energy just to walk the twelve feet from her desk to the door.

"I've got to ask: Where did you get the information to write this short story?" she asked, smiling.

"It was nothing more than a dream that's been in my head for the past six weeks," I replied, pushing the door open.

I left my teacher sitting there, looking at me as if I had just told the biggest lie this side of the Mississippi River. And as I left the class and the school behind me, peddling like mad to get home, I knew it would be a matter of moments, hours, or possibly days before she talked to my parents about entering the story into the summer contest. She'd have to talk to them to get their approval. It would do nothing but freak my mother out. How dare I have such dreams! Such nightmares! But I was a teenager, or at least I would be in several days; my dreams had evolved into much more than what they used to be.

03

I was counting down the days until my thirteenth birthday, which was now only six days away. I couldn't wait.

I laughed, thinking about my sisters doing all the farm work this summer.

Life wasn't all bad. I had three best friends, good parents, the best dog in the world, and three crazy, bratty sisters.

The girls were allowed to sleep late, but not me. I was the one to help Dad out on our small farm.

Dad and I were always up before the sun rose.

I had to gather eggs, feed the pigs and the three horses, and milk the three cows that always seemed to hang out down by the pond where I usually swam in the afternoons.

The cows walked quickly away from me when they saw me lugging the little red wagon with the milk pails and a little stool. I pulled that little red wagon all over the place many times looking for those unruly cows. It took me more than an hour just to catch up with the cows, slip a rope around their necks and tie them to a tree just to milk them. I got the feeling they were laughing at me some days.

I overheard my parents talking one evening. OK, maybe I was eavesdropping. It was at times the only way to get firsthand knowledge for some of my stories. My two older sisters were in the back room screaming at each other over what dress Tammy should wear. They'd be at it for hours, or until Mom called us to dinner.

My oldest cousin, Kyle, was down visiting. He had gotten two weeks off from college in Baton Rouge. He considers my parents more like his brother and sister. I never heard him call either of them *aunt* or *uncle*. He always called them by their first names.

I liked Kyle. He was like the older brother I'd never had. I liked that he talked to me as if I were an adult.

He looked like a rich city man with his newly styled haircut and his uptown clothes. He was as tall as my dad and had blond hair and blue eyes and a laugh that made you feel good to be around him.

The gift I loved the most was the small rat terrier bluetick hound dog he'd given me for my ninth birthday. I'd named him Butch. He was my best friend. He'd usually follow me everywhere, except to school and into the pond. He despised water.

04

Mom, Dad, and Kyle had just walked in through the back door as the girls were carrying on at the back of the house. I could have easily slipped out the front door, but eavesdropping was a lot more fun. I dropped onto the floor and ducked behind the couch. There was something about hearing adults talking when you weren't supposed to that set your heart slamming in your chest. I lay there on my back staring up at the ceiling.

"So tell me, Kyle, how much longer do you have to go to college till you get your degree?" Mom asked as she rocked in the old rocker my grandfather had made for her before I was born.

"Well, Jenny," Kyle said, stopping for a second to choke on the cigarette smoke my father no doubt blew in his direction.

"This is my last semester. I've only got four weeks until I get my medical degree."

Kyle was the first member of this entire family to go to college.

"What about a job?" Dad asked.

"I've already got three different offers in three different states," Kyle said proudly.

I was hoping that one of them was in the state of Louisiana. I'd hate to see Kyle move far away.

"Well, where are they?" Dad asked.

"One of them is in Chicago, one is in New Orleans, and the last one is in Denver, Colorado."

"Denver?" Mom asked.

"Yeah, they just built one of the newest children's hospitals up there. All three offers are for children's hospitals."

My cousin the doctor.

The smoke from my dad's cigarette was falling to the floor. I had to blow it back up or choke on it.

"I sure hope you think about taking the offer in New Orleans. It would break Ryan's heart if you moved so far away. You've got that boy spoiled," Mom said.

"None of the positions will be open 'til the first of the year, so I've got the entire summer to think on it. The hospital in Denver is offering the highest salary, then Chicago, then New Orleans."

"Go where the big money is," Dad said.

I shook my head back and forth while blowing the smoke away from my nostrils. *Don't tell him that*, I thought.

"There's something I want to ask the both of you." Kyle said, keeping his voice low.

"Well, speak up," Dad said.

05

"All right, but let's keep our voices low," Kyle said above a whisper.

"Why?" Momma asked.

"I don't want the girls to find out, and I want it to be a surprise for Ryan."

A surprise for me! I was all for that. What is it? I wanted to shout. Just then I noticed a spider free floating toward me.

"Where is Ryan by the way?" Kyle asked.

"He's probably down at the pond with Butch. I swear that dog is his shadow," Mom said lowering her voice.

I shook my head back and forth as this spider was dropping itself through the haze of cigarette smoke on an invisible string of web from the ceiling above me. It was coming though the smoke straight toward my forehead. It was now below the top edge of the couch and dropping fast. I blew at it, and it went swinging psychotically back and forth in the air right between my eyes. I swear it was laughing at me.

"Well, what is it?" Mom asked, keeping her voice low.

"Yeah, what do you want?" I mouthed to the spider as it came closer to me. I could feel its furry little body against the bridge of my nose even though it hadn't yet touched my skin.

The spider was swinging back and forth, its beady eyes locked somewhere on my shirt. It came closer. I was wishing my sisters were all tied up watching the spider dangle above them. I reached up and flicked it in midair. It went flying over the edge of the couch.

"I'll have the entire summer free. One of my friends from college wants me to hang out with him. His father owns a houseboat down on the Atchafalaya Basin. His father is allowing him to use the houseboat for the entire summer. He's invited me to spend the summer down there as well," Kyle said, all in one breath.

"And you want Ryan to come down there with you for the summer, right?" Dad asked.

I know that tone, and it usually sounds like a no.

"Yes."

Yes, yes, yesssssssss, please Lord up in Heaven, make them both say yes, I prayed as the spider started crawling swiftly back over the couch. It was dead set on my shirt or my face for some reason. I could almost hear it laughing at me. "I'm gonna bite ya," I heard its still, small voice on the air.

"That's the swamps?" Mom said with concern in her voice. She knew it was; we all did.

"Yeah, it is, but you know I'll keep an eye on him."

"Does this friend of yours have a name?" Dad asked.

"Dennis Boudreaux."

"How long do you plan on keeping my son out there in the swamps?" Dad asked.

"Well I'd come and get him on his birthday, and we'd be back by the end of August."

That sounded fair to me I thought as the spider came closer.

"I'm gonna need an address, and a phone number to this friend's parents, in case something happens. I'm gonna want you to call here at this house at least once a week. And I expect you to be there with Ryan. I'm gonna want to talk to the both of ya."

"Seriously, you know I'll guard him with my life."

"I don't like the tone in your voice. Don't get an attitude. Don't forget your mother is still my sister."

"Yes, ma'am. I'm sorry."

Yes, don't mess it up, before they even say yes, I wanted to shout over the top of the couch.

"I will not let you haul my son to the swamps for the entire summer and not be able to talk to him. You have a car; you'll need to go to some town for groceries and supplies, will you not?"

"Yes, ma'am."

"They gonna have a payphone. I'll expect a phone call at least every eight to ten days, or the days you and your friend go to some nearby payphone. There are a million things out there that could eat or kill the both of ya. Am I clear on this one rule?" It was mom's turn to pace the floor between the kitchen and the living room, which she did when she was nervous or angry.

"Yes. Every eight to ten days or on the grocery run I'll have Ryan on the phone with you."

06

"That's over two months," Mom said, just above a whisper.

"Let me and Jenny talk it over for a few minutes," Dad said while getting out of his chair.

"Sure thing, I'll go tell the girls hi," Kyle said, getting up from the couch.

I could hear his footsteps echoing down the hallway as he left the living room. I wish my parents would just say yes. My dad always paced back and forth in front of the couch when he was thinking about things getting in the way of farm work. And if I was gone for over two months, that was getting in the way of farm work.

"I don't know if I like the idea of Ryan being down in the swamps for over two months," Mom started, keeping her voice low.

"Kyle is a responsible young man, but the thought of one of them alligators eating my boy scares the daylights out of me. I couldn't live with myself if something like that happened to my baby."

Baby? I ain't no baby. I am going on thirteen years old.

"You know Ryan and I have come across a few gators in the past several years on our own fishing trips out at Whiskey Bay, which is part of the Atchafalaya Basin. The boy is not afraid of gators at all. He knows how dangerous they are, and he knows how to use that rifle we gave him last year. I'm not worried about the swamps at all. I trust Kyle to take good care of Ryan, but ..."

He must have taken several puffs on his cigarette. I could see a new haze coming toward me, and I almost choked as the spider crept closer to my face. I had lost all visual of the spider a moment before; I found myself on the edge of every word my parents were saying about me.

"I'm afraid I'll need his help on the farm," Dad said.

It sounded like I wasn't going to be going; I did what any old twelve-year-old boy would have done with three bratty sisters that never did any farm work—I almost started crying.

"Well," Momma started to say, "if you think Ryan will be safe out there in the swamps, the girls can help out with the farm work this summer."

I wanted to jump up and kiss my mother.

"I never thought about them," Dad said quietly.

Why not, I thought to myself.

"Yes, I think it will do the girls some good to do some work this summer. It will teach them some responsibility." Mom must have sat back down. Her echoing footsteps on the old floors faded.

"All right, we'll let him go."

I wanted to jump up and kiss my father.

I was going to spend the entire summer in the swamps.

My sisters would have to work the farm. Life was grand.

07

After what seemed like ages, Kyle and my parents walked out the back door to Kyle's car. I just knew their conversation was about me. I darted out the front door and ran toward the barn. I found Butch up in the hayloft.

How he got up there was beyond me. He had my sister's cat, Brownie, cornered. Brownie's back was hunched up high, spitting this way and that. She was ready for a fight. Butch kept edging closer and closer to Brownie, backing her farther up into the corner.

"How did you get up here, boy?" I asked while grabbing his collar to keep him from jumping on poor old Brownie.

Brownie kept hissing and scratching the air in front of Butch. I could see through the open barn door at the top of the loft that Kyle was getting into his car.

"Lookie here, Butch. I don't know how you managed to get up here, but if Kyle leaves, and I don't get to tell him goodbye, you will not be going to the swamps with me this summer."

I kept dragging Butch to the edge of the loft. I noticed the hay used for feeding the cows and the horses was piled high. I shoved Butch over the side then jumped right after him. Sliding my hand under his collar, we walked quickly out into the yard. Mom and Dad went back into the house. Kyle was driving off but stopped when he saw us running up to the back of the car.

"Hey, Champ, I was wondering where you were. I've been here for over an hour now. I've got to be getting on the road, but I'll be back for your birthday. I've got a surprise for you. I want you to be good until I get back. Stay out of trouble. Don't fight with your sisters."

Butch and I stood there as he drove off, waving until long after his car had faded from view.

08

The days flew by, and I was considered the perfect angel around the house, and I was sure my parents probably knew I was being good for something. My grades at school were better than average, despite the one D I got on my report card. I had passed for the year. To me that was all that mattered. Had I failed there would be no getting away from the farm work all summer.

I kept waiting to hear something from my teacher about the short story I wrote for class, but she didn't call or stop by the house to speak to me or my parents about it. I was so busy with the farm work and writing in my journal that I didn't think about anything else other than my escape to the swamps.

Six more days 'til my birthday. School was out. I was counting down the days 'til I was a full-fledged "Swampin-Cajun Boy."

I'd love to see the looks on my sisters' faces when they had to do it all. I could just hear Charlene: "No, no, these hands are not touching that cow." And Marie, being the oldest, would say, "Well I am the oldest, so you better do it, or I'll shove you under the cow.

Sometimes, my sisters were OK, but that was seldom. I couldn't understand why my mother had to have three of them. Tammy, being only three years of age, would get out of most of the farm work.

Every day I would tell Butch where Kyle was taking me. He'd just stare straight ahead or fall over and play dead. He wasn't like normal hound dogs that enjoyed hunting. The only kind of hunting Butch enjoyed was stalking my sister's cat or chasing Momma's prized laying hens.

"Go out in the fields and tell your daddy that supper will be ready in about half an hour, and don't mess around either; there is some bad weather moving in."

"Yes, ma'am, I won't," I said, as I walked out the kitchen door. I finally came up to my dad's tractor. But he wasn't there. The engine on the tractor was still running. I climbed up in the tractor and shut the engine off.

Looking out to my left I spotted my father running near the end of the tractor. He was running straight toward one of our cows lying on her side. The cows never roamed these parts of the fields. I jumped down from the tractor, grabbed Butch's leash, then started running toward my father.

I recognized the cow as Elsie. She had one big black spot on her forehead. We had given our three cows names a long time back. Marie had named one Eloise; Charlene had named one Clarisse, and I had named this one Elsie. Elsie turned out to be one of our best milking cows.

"What happened to her?" I asked short of breath.

"She caught her foot in that hole," Dad said, pointing to a small hole directly behind Elsie's left leg. Her leg was all twisted, the bone sticking through the fur, and she was moaning something awful and bleeding heavily from behind her rear legs. "Ryan, I want you to run to the house and get my shotgun."

"Why?" I asked, knowing full well in my twelve-year-old mind why he wanted it. The tears ran salty over my lips.

"I'm afraid she has broken her leg, and there's just too much blood. She's suffering awfully bad." Dad's voice was just above a whisper, and his hands were covered in Elsie's blood.

"Can't you fix it? Can't you stop the bleeding?" I asked hoarsely.

"No, I can't fix it. Elsie has been on her last legs for a long while now. I'm going to have to shoot her."

"No! I won't let *you kill Elsie!*" I hissed at my father through my tears.

09

The wind started to whip through the fields, bringing with it the smell of rain not far behind. Lightning lit up the sky, and thunder rolled. It was a little after six, but it was dark as if it were midnight.

"I have no other choice; now you had better run to the house and get my shotgun, before this storm starts."

My father stood and looked off into the distance.

"I won't go!" I said, defiantly licking the tears.

"Look here young man," Dad said while grabbing me and shaking me. "You do what I tell you to do! Do you understand me?"

He forced me to look him in the eyes. I could see the tears locked up in the corner of his eyes as well.

"Look, Son, Elsie is suffering, and there is no other way of helping her. She has lived a long life, and it would be wrong of us to leave her in all this pain. I don't want to shoot her, but you have lived on a farm your entire life, and you know this must be done. Now run to the house and get my gun. You tell your mother what has happened, and hurry right back."

With tears running down my face, I ran toward the house.

"Momma! *Momma*!" I shouted, running into the kitchen. I stood there shaking and gasping for breath.

"What's the matter?" she asked.

The worry lines creased her face when she saw my bloodshot eyes and my tear-streaked face.

"What's wrong? Where's your father?" She asked, just about on the verge of tears herself.

I couldn't answer her; I was still shocked that my father wanted to shoot Elsie.

"Answer me, young man?" Her voice was on the rise.

"He's out in the fields with Elsie. She's hurt something awful. She's bleeding, and her leg is all twisted and broken. Daddy says he's got to shoot her! He told me … to, to get his shotgun!"

"Poor Elsie," Mom said in a low voice.

It was easy to see she was trying not to cry in front of me. She ran to the bedroom to get Dad's shotgun.

Marie and Charlene appeared in the doorway to their bedroom. They both had tears caught up in their eyes. They heard what I said; they knew it as well. We all loved Elsie.

"What happened to Elsie?" Charlene asked in between sobs.

"She fell and broke her leg out in the field," I said while looking down at the floor.

My throat felt dry and raw.

Mom came back to the kitchen with Dad's shotgun and laid it on the table. She opened the pantry in the right-hand corner of the kitchen.

That's where dad kept the shells for all his guns. It was so high up that Momma had to tiptoe while standing on one of the kitchen chairs. She closed the pantry, shoved the chair back under the table, and walked toward me all in one step. She handed me the shotgun and the shells.

"Put these shells in your pocket. Hurry up, and get back before this storm starts."

"It's the best thing to do for her, Ryan. You know that, don't you, Son? Elsie has had a long life, and she's been sick for a while, and if she is bleeding as bad as you said, it's the fastest way to end her pain." Mom held my chin in her hand for a moment.

"I don't understand why he has to shoot her." I bit my lip to keep any more tears from coming, but I did understand. I just didn't want her life to end.

"Oh, honey, I'm so sorry about poor Elsie. There's just no way of helping her. If your dad doesn't do it now, she'll just die slowly. She's got to be suffering pretty bad. I know it's hard for you kids to understand."

"Nobody put Uncle Larry down when he broke his leg last year," Charlene cried.

"Honey, this is far worse than a broken leg, and we all know it."

"Now," Momma said, as she turned back to me, "I want you to run as fast as you can and give those shells and that gun to your father."

She pulled me into that motherly hug of hers.

"Hurry up and get back to the house; it's going to be a bad storm."

10

I ran out of the kitchen and tore through the back yard. Butch was barking like mad as I ran past his doghouse. I thought about bringing him with me but decided against it. He would just tangle things up.

The clouds looked like massive cotton balls, smeared in black ink. I had never seen it this dark before in my life. It seemed to get darker with every step. It was so dark I soon realized I was lost. I couldn't see my dad, Elsie, or the tractor anywhere.

"Daddy! Daddy!" I yelled as loud as I could.

My voice swam in one huge circle and slammed right back into my eardrums.

"*Daddy!*" I yelled at the top of my lungs.

The wind started howling like a wild, demonic ghost dancing at a tent revival.

Just the thought of it gave me the chills. I didn't think it could have gotten any darker than it already was. I stood frozen as a sudden wave of fear swept over me.

"Oh, God, please help me find my dad."

I turned around fixing to run back to the house, but the house was nowhere to be seen. It was like being in one of the horror novels I liked reading. I was standing in total darkness, and I was scared to death. My teeth were chattering against the bite of the wind.

"*Daddy!*" I shouted as loud as I could.

A massive streak of lightning struck, setting the darkness ablaze with light for a moment. I had to close my eyes to its brilliance.

And then the thunder struck so loud that it sounded like dynamite in the sky. I caught sight of our tractor. It was no more than ten feet behind me. I ran in that direction as the blackness sucked up the night again.

I had been taught to drive this tractor back when I was seven. I could hardly reach the pedals on the floor, but I knew how to drive it. I turned the engine on, switched the lights on bright and turned the tractor completely around.

I drove the tractor forward about ten feet, quickly jumped down and handed the gun and the shells to my dad. He loaded the shotgun, cocked it, and took aim.

"No! Wait a minute; please let me tell her bye!" I begged as tears burned my vision.

He looked at me for a moment, then down at Elsie, as he held the gun to her head. "Please!"

"Make it fast, Son, we've got to get back to the house before this storm starts," Dad said with tears in his eyes.

"Good-bye, old girl," I whispered in her ear, wrapping my arms around her big neck. She may have only been a cow, but she had been a friend and part of our family.

"Why did you have to fall and break your leg?" I cried.

Elsie kept moaning in pain. I could see tears caught up in her big brown eyes.

"Come on, Son. I want you to wait at the tractor. I'm real sorry it has to be this way." He hugged my neck.

I knew deep down my father didn't want to put Elsie down, but I knew it had to be done. I climbed up onto the tractor, and as I reached the top step, I heard the shot. He was right behind me.

11

I sat on the fender over the wheel left of where my father sat driving the tractor all the way back to the farm. Neither of us said a word. I stared straight ahead into the darkness; big silent tears streaked my face.

The second we drove up to the back of the barn, it started to rain softly, as if the rain were afraid of the dark and didn't want to fall. There was more wind than anything, and as fast as the rain started, it stopped.

"Hurry up and check on the other animals while I put the tractor away," Dad yelled at me over the roar of the engine and the wind.

I jumped down from the tractor and ran around to the front of the barn. The animals were safely in their pens but for Elsie.

Dad parked the tractor in the back of the barn. It had grown silent and pitch black.

"I don't like the looks of this weather," Dad said, in a tone I had never heard before. He stood there looking back toward the field where we had left Elsie.

"What's the matter?" I peered out into the darkness, trying to see what my Dad saw.

"Let's go, Ryan!" He shouted at the top of his lungs, as the wind started up like a blazing fire gone out of control. "There's a tornado coming!"

"*Jenny!*" Dad shouted, as we ran into the kitchen.

"Grab the girls; there's a tornado coming."

"Get to the bathroom!" Dad yelled at everyone. He ran to the bedroom and yanked the mattress from the bed.

Mom got in the tub with my three sisters as Dad practically threw the mattress over them. The moment he did, I ran from the back hall area.

"Ryan! Get back here!" I heard my father yell, but I ran even faster.

"I'm not gonna leave Butch out there by himself!" I screamed.

The wind slammed the back door shut. I couldn't have been more than twenty feet from the house, but as I turned to look back, it might have been a hundred feet or more.

My heart froze in my chest; the air in my lungs seemed caught up in the back of my throat as a dark funnel of clouds headed straight toward our small farm. I could hardly see it as it whipped about against the blackness.

Butch was barking like mad. The house, the farm, my dad's voice, everything was lost to the roaring wind. I don't know how I made it to Butch's doghouse, but I did.

He was at the end of his leash barking like crazy at the roaring wind that was coming into the chicken yard. I grabbed Butch by the collar and yanked him into the doghouse as the wind got louder, the sky grew darker, and the doghouse started to tremble.

I unhooked Butch from his twenty-foot chain, pulled him tight to me and held on for life. It was a big doghouse, and I crab-crawled sideways and backward, inside, pulling Butch into the back corner with me. My back pressed firmly into the wood, my eyes glued to the open doorway. The doghouse and the ground started to shake violently, and I was struck dumb at how there seemed to be a freight train suddenly screaming through our yard.

It was beyond loud, and I was scared to death.

12

"Stay with me, old boy!" I whispered. I knew somewhere in the back of my mind that it would be a matter of seconds before we left the ground like Dorothy's house in the *Wizard of Oz.*

Suddenly, out of nowhere, Buttercup, one of Momma's hens, appeared in the open doorway of the doghouse.

She looked as if she would fly away if she could. Her back was toward me, and she was clucking angrily at the wind.

I reached out and snatched her, yanking her to me. Butch, the hen, and I were silent as the doghouse rose from the ground for only a moment, then slammed back to the ground. The doghouse started sliding along the dirt yard. I closed my eyes and held on tight to Butch and my mom's hen. The doghouse tipped over on its side, and we went tumbling, like a tumbleweed blowing in the desert.

"It's OK; we're all OK," I said to the hen. Butch licked my face and started barking. The doghouse had landed back upright, in one piece, clear out in the field.

I got out, stood up, and looked around. Butch scrambled out of the doghouse. The darkness had evaporated, and the stars and the moon were out. I looked around and realized we were clear out in the field where Elsie was, but she was nowhere to be seen.

The hen was very calm. I tightened my grip around the hen, and we started running toward the farm. Butch was right on my heels. I was amazed at how bright the moon and stars all were!

I saw that the front roof to the porch had been torn from the house and was totally blocking the front door. There was no way my family could get out that way. The back door was blocked by one of the huge oak trees that had been uprooted from our back yard. The oak tree was lying against the back of the house, and all the roots were lying up against the back door.

"Momma! Daddy! Are you guys all right in there?" I shouted, as Butch started barking.

"Oh, Ryan!" Momma cried. "Are you OK, Son?"

"I'm OK."

"Son, I can't get this door open," Dad said.

"The oak tree is lying against the house. Dad, what'll I do? I can't move this tree by myself."

Butch started pawing at the tree, and then he started barking like crazy.

"Hang on. I can't hear you. Stop!" I commanded.

"How am I gonna move this tree?"

"Can you hear me OK?" Dad was speaking to me from the small kitchen window.

"Yes, sir, I can hear you."

"I want you to get the tractor, get the chains I keep in the tool shed. Wrap the chains around the base of the tree. Latch it onto the ball on the back of the tractor and pull the tree away. Do you think you can do all of that?"

"Sure."

It sounded all easy enough. I wanted to tell them all to just climb out through the windows, but I knew for a fact that all the old, heavy wood frame window screens were nailed in tight. We had secured them in last year, and now my family was trapped. Some of the huge branches up against the back of the house lay across some of the windows like giant twisted witches' fingers, scratching the night sky. It was twisted indeed, and I wrote it all down in my mind so that I could put it to paper later.

13

I felt ten feet tall when it came to driving the tractor. It sounded easy enough; however, as I walked to the tool shed, it was easy to see it wasn't there. Where it normally stood, only the foundation remained. There were no tools, no chains, no shed, no nothing. I ran around the yard searching for some of the chains, but it was no use.

"Dad!" I screamed, short of breath. "The tool shed isn't there anymore! The tornado took off with it. I can't find the chains anywhere."

Dad was quiet for a long moment.

"All right. Ryan, are you listening to me, Son?"

"Yes, sir, I'm right here."

"You know where we keep all the ropes at up in the loft?"

"Yes, sir, I know right where they are." I ran back to the barn.

I climbed up into the loft. The entire roof of the barn was gone.

After searching for a few minutes, I finally found the rope under some hay. I was surprised it hadn't blown away like everything else. I looked down to notice all the animals in their pens. They all looked spooked, but they were there. I thought about poor Elsie, as I looked down at Eloise and Clarisse. The ropes were too much for me to carry, so I shoved it all over the side of the loft.

Dragging the rope behind me, I hauled it over to the tree lying up against the house, then ran back to the rear section of the barn where the tractor was parked. The walls and the ceiling above the tractor were gone.

I jumped up on the tractor, turned the engine on, and started toward the house. On the way to the house from the back of the barn, I should have passed right next to Momma's chicken coop.

I shook my head, surprised it wasn't there. The fence that made up the chicken yard was all that was left. No chickens were anywhere to be seen.

Thank the Lord no major damage was done to the house.

I had to move the tractor back and forth several times to get it in place. I jumped down and went to work tying the rope around the base of the tree, then the other end around the back of the tractor. The tractor was steady and strong as I drove it forward, pulling the tree away from the house.

The door to the kitchen opened, and we all hugged one another. I was surprised that neither of my parents scolded me for running after Butch. Had I not run after him, we'd have all been trapped in the house.

Dad turned the tractor engine off, and we walked around the yard inspecting the damage. Momma gasped when she noticed the chicken coop and their yard had been destroyed. Nothing was in sight but twisted chicken wire. Dad cursed up a storm when he saw the damage done to the barn.

"Let's go inside," Dad said.

"I'm sure we'll find more damage in the morning."

We walked up to the back of the house. My sisters were screaming for Brownie; he was found sitting in the bathroom sink.

"It's a miracle," Momma said.

No harm had come to the house at all, other than the front porch. In fact, the chicken was still roasting in the oven.

"It sure is a miracle," Dad said, helping to set the table.

"Let us give thanks," Momma said, while sitting down next to Dad.

"Dear Lord, we want to thank you for saving our lives this day. Thank you that we still have a roof over our heads and food on our table. Amen," Momma said.

"Amen," we all whispered.

14

The next five days were spent cleaning up and repairing the damage from the tornado. It seemed that our farm was the only farm in the parish that had been touched by the tornado. Friends, neighbors, and relatives chipped in to help us with the rebuilding of the barn.

Within two days, the barn had a new roof, and the section where the tractor had been kept had been enlarged to twice its size.

Momma got a brand-new chicken coop, a dozen new laying hens, a dozen baby chicks, and one very old rooster. Buttercup, the hen that survived it all, became Momma's pet. She started carrying it around like a little dog and even brought it into the house at times. Buttercup was special, and she was treated like royalty.

Even the size of the chicken yard was enlarged.

Most of Dad's tools were found out in the field; some of them had been blown clear down to the pond.

The tornado must have blown Elise's body into another parish for we never could find her.

Butch was up to his old habits again, chasing Brownie from one end of the yard to the next.

June 12th had finally come. Momma and the girls had gone to town to do the weekly grocery shopping. Dad was out in the fields working on the tractor. He said this one could be an all-day job. It was going on nine in the morning, and he had been working on it since seven.

To everyone else it was a normal day, but to me, it was the day I would become a free man.

Free from all the farm work for the entire summer. I had gotten up even earlier than usual on this day. I had all my farm work done at eight this morning. It was just about nine when I sat down to a big bowl of cornflakes. That was good, so I sat there and had another. I was a growing man; I had to have my cornflakes.

I knew Momma would have yelled at me for eating so much, but Momma wasn't there.

I had the entire day to myself. What to do, what to do. Whenever Momma and the girls went to town, they usually stopped off for a visit at taunt Charlotte and uncle Larry's house. I'm glad I wasn't there. I could just picture myself on the front porch with Rachael, Michael, Darla, Charlene, Marie, and Tammy. No way. Rachael, Michael, and Darla were my three other cousins. It was a shame uncle Larry had to have three girls. I don't know how he stood it not having a son.

I was happy to be here, could care less if I ever went into town. I was out here on the farm and going to the pond just about every day.

15

I knew Kyle wouldn't be here to pick me up till late in the afternoon. It was only a quarter to ten in the morning, a very hot muggy morning. The weatherman on the radio said it was going to be in the high nineties, possibly even hundred degrees.

I went to the bathroom searching for one of Momma's oldest towels. Finding one, I headed for the kitchen door. I stood on the back porch, looked out toward the field, and then I turned around and went back inside. I decided to fix Dad a tall glass of iced tea.

I poured the tea into one of Momma's empty canning jars, added some ice cubes, and then screwed the lid on tight.

Butch was still sitting by the oak tree, straining his fool neck to see where Brownie had gone. I snuck up behind him and yelled as loud as I could. Butch fell over, as if he just had a heart attack.

"It's time to give it up old boy. Brownie doesn't want to be seen. Come on; let's go to the pond."

Butch lay there with all four legs sticking straight up, his eyes shut tight, and his tail thumping against the ground.

"Good, you keep your eyes closed," I whispered to myself. I grabbed his leash, ran over to the oak tree, snuck quietly upon him, and attached the leash to his collar before he had the chance to get up.

"Gotcha! Come on, old boy. Let's go to the pond." I only got a couple of feet when I realized that Butch wasn't following me. He was still playing dead, lying there with all four legs sticking straight up in the air like a possum hit by a car.

"I promise you won't have to go in the water." Still he didn't move.

"*Food!*" I yelled at Butch.

He jerked to life and flipped over on all fours. That was about the only thing that got him going when he was playing dead.

The barn was right there in front of us. That's where his dog food was kept, right inside the barn door. I opened the barn door and took the old, rusted metal pot from the dog food and filled my pockets full. I knew Butch would follow me.

I dumped a handful of dog food on the ground, and he swallowed it in one gulp. He knew my pockets were full of dog food. He could smell it. He kept licking at my pockets.

"You'll get it when we get to the pond," I said as I pushed his nose away.

16

After ten minutes of walking, we finally came up to my dad's tractor. He was on top of the engine peering down at something. His clothes were caked in oil and his hands and face were almost black from the oil and dirt.

"Darn thing," I heard him say with disgust.

"I brought you some iced tea," I said.

"Thanks, Son." He gulped half of it down in one swig.

"So, where are you off to?"

"I've finished all the farm work, and Butch and I are headed down to the pond for the rest of the day."

"Sounds like fun. I'd go, but this tractor has more problems than I know what to do with."

"Have your mother and the girls come back yet?" Dad asked, as he chugged down the last of the tea.

"No, Mom said something about going to visit Taunt Charlotte and Uncle Larry." I got down from the tractor and grabbed Butch's leash.

"They should be gone for the rest of the day. Why didn't you go with them?"

"Please, Dad, don't tell me you'd want to be around all those girls."

"I don't much blame you; girls were not top of my list of things to do when I was your age either.

"Well, you had better get on to that pond," Dad said with a wink in his eye.

I turned to leave.

"Oh, Son,"

"Yeah, Dad."

"Happy birthday, Son."

"Thanks Dad."

Butch started to pull back as we went down the hill through the thick line of pine trees. He followed me to the shoreline though, mainly because I had fed him all the way down the hill, and he knew my pockets were full of dog food.

By the time we got to the water's edge, my pockets were empty. "Don't worry I don't plan on dragging you in the water." I bent over to rub Butch in between the ears. He fell over and played dead, and I rubbed his stomach for a few minutes. He always loved that. I took his leash off, and he rolled over and went to sleep.

"I swear you're the laziest dog I've ever seen in my whole life."

I spread my clothes out on the ground, laid the towel down on top of them and laid down, and like Butch, I was asleep in minutes.

"You won't be able to sit on that behind for a month if you sleep out here in the sun much longer," Kyle said as he walked down the small embankment toward me.

"How long have you been here?" I asked, as I jumped up and into the rest of my clothes.

"I just got here. Your dad said you were out here. And, no, I wasn't followed by your sisters."

Kyle bent over to pet Butch. He started thumping his tail hard against the ground.

"What time is it?" I asked.

"It's going on five." I just wanted to blurt out I knew all about the swamp trip, but I kept my mouth shut.

"We better get back to the house. You know …," Kyle started to say, but then he must have changed his mind. We were both silent for the moment.

"I'm waiting."

"It can wait."

"So, what's your trick at making this lazy old dog follow us?"

"Bend over and yell "*food*," at him. Trust me it works every time."

Kyle bent over and yelled "food," at Butch. He sprang to life, jumped to his feet, and took off for the farm, leaving us behind. We both doubled over with laughter and started back to the house.

17

"I don't know about you, but I am starving. Your mom is cooking spaghetti and meatballs, and it smelled pretty good when I left the house to come down here to get you."

"My favorite," I said as we started across the fields toward the farm.

"So tell me, what have you been up to since last I saw you?"

"Nothing really. Just helping out with the farm and swimming as much as possible and avoiding my sisters. I passed to the seventh grade."

"You know we had a tornado come through here this past week," I told him.

"Yeah, I'm sorry I wasn't around, but I was in the middle of some major meetings about what I am to do with the rest of my life."

"So tell me what happened. I heard you were the hero around here."

Kyle was silent, and I talked the entire way back to the farm.

"Wow, that's quite a tale. I like the part about the hen appearing in the doorway. I hope you wrote it all down."

"Every single word is in my journal you gave me for Christmas."

"Hey, let's go take a look at the new and improved barn."

"I thought you were starving?"

"I was, I mean, I am, but it can wait for a few minutes."

"All right."

As I went to open the barn door, Kyle placed his hand on my shoulder.

"Hey, Champ."

"Yeah, what?" I asked, turning to face him.

"Happy birthday."

18

"*H*appy birthday!" Everyone shouted as the barn door swung open. They had all this planned for me.

Taunt Charlotte and Uncle Larry were there with their three girls. My grandparents on my father's side and my mother's side were there too. Even two of my best friends from school had shown up for a change.

Mom had baked a triple decker chocolate cake with banana filling. The table looked heavenly, with all the cupcakes and homemade chocolate chip cookies, surrounding a big punch bowl.

"Happy birthday, Ryan," Mom said, as she pulled me into that motherly hug of hers. Then everyone sang "Happy Birthday."

My grandparents on both sides gave me a card with five bucks in it. Ten bucks was the most money this thirteen-year-old boy had ever had. I could go to town and then some on ten dollars.

"This is from all three of us," Marie said, as she handed me a red package.

"We all chipped in for the material," Charlene said as I leaned in to open it.

"Shut your mouth, dummy," Marie hissed.

"Sorry, I forgot," Charlene said.

"Open it! Open it!" Tammy said excitedly.

"Here, you want to help me open it?" I asked, bending over next to her. Tammy shook her head yes and quickly yanked the package out of my hands and ripped it open, as if it were hers and not mine. It was a bright red pair of swimming shorts.

"I made them myself!" Marie said proudly.

"I helped," Charlene said.

"Momma made them," Tammy cried.

"Thanks," I said. I think it was the first time I had ever thanked my sisters for anything.

"Now you don't have to go skinny dipping anymore," Marie whispered in my ear.

Taunt Charlotte and Uncle Larry gave me a red baseball cap.

"That's from us too," little Darla cried.

"Thank you; I love it."

"Happy birthday, Son," Dad said, as he handed me a brand-new fishing rod with a bright red bow wrapped around the end. "It was kind of hard to wrap."

"Thanks, Dad and Mom, I love it."

"You're going to need that where you're going," Dad said, winking at Kyle.

"Ryan, I talked it over with your parents, and they've both agreed to let you go with me." Kyle looked up at Dad.

"Go with you where?" I tried to act surprised. I was ready to jump in Kyle's car and take off right then.

"I'm going to be spending the entire summer in the Atchafalaya Basin with a friend on a houseboat. And you, my dear boy, are coming with me; that is, if you want to?"

"That's the swamps, right?" I was about ready to jump out of my skin.

"It's the largest swamp in the United States," said Uncle Larry.

"The entire summer! When do we leave?" I asked.

Kyle looked over at my mom.

"As soon as you get packed," said Mom.

"Go on and pack," Dad said while holding onto my fishing rod.

"Is it all right if I bring Timmy and Bobby to my room to help me pack?"

"Sure, just don't drag dirt in my house," Momma said. The three of us ran to my bedroom.

"You lucky dog," Bobby said, as we walked into my bedroom.

"I've known about it since Easter," I said, pulling my duffle bag from the back of the closet. I had packed it early this morning.

"You're packed already?" Timmy asked, as I sat down on the bed.

"I started packing it last week and finished last night. Come here and sit down, and let me tell you all about it."

Both my friends sat on the bed, and I told them the entire story of how I was eavesdropping behind the couch listening to my parents and Kyle and the spider.

"Man, ya crazy," Timmy said.

"I would have been caught," said Bobby.

19

Both of my older sisters suddenly developed a bad attitude toward me. I could care less for I wouldn't have to see either of their faces for well over sixty days.

"You two boys hop in the car," Uncle Larry said to my friends.

"You're OK with taking them back to town?" Mom asked.

"Sure, they're good boys," Uncle Larry said. He slammed the car door, started the engine, and drove off. I could tell Uncle Larry wanted a son just by the sound of his voice.

It was a little after six when we all sat down to Mom's good old spaghetti and meatballs.

"Kyle, would you mind saying 'Grace'?" Mom asked while setting an ice-cold pitcher of lemonade on the table.

Everyone bowed their heads.

"Lord bless this food and everyone at this table, and let us never pass those up that are less fortunate than ourselves, Amen."

"Amen," said Dad. As soon as Kyle finished, everyone started talking at once.

"That was a short prayer but very nice," said Mom.

"Thanks," said Kyle.

"I sure ain't gonna be shoveling no cow droppings, no ma'am I ain't," Charlene said.

"You wanna bet," said Marie.

"The two of you will be helping out with all the farm work this summer while your brother is away," Dad said firmly.

"Well, it's not fair that he should be able to go away for the entire summer," Marie spat with a twisted grin on her face.

"That is enough," Momma snapped.

20

I knew Marie and Charlene were both jealous at the moment, but I just didn't care. I was a free man for the entire summer and for the first summer ever.

Tammy could have cared less.

I inhaled my plate of food. I was ready to leave; I had been ready to leave for more than two weeks now. I looked over at Kyle.

"Well, you guys had better get on the road," Dad said.

"I guess so," Kyle replied.

"I know it's a drive from here," Dad said.

"Yes! *Yes!* Let's get out of here," I wanted to shout.

"You all packed?" Kyle asked me, looking over at Momma.

"Yep," I said while smiling broadly at my sisters. You could almost see the steam coming out of their ears (except for Tammy.)

Kyle slipped his arms around my mom's neck. "Now don't you worry one bit about Ryan. I love him like a little brother, and I promise to keep a close eye on him. I'll call here so he can talk with you at least three or four times a month unless we can't make it to a payphone."

"I know you will, Kyle. I trust you." They hugged one another for a moment.

She walked over to me and gave me that motherly hug that made a kid feel good inside.

"I want you to have a good time out there, but you had better mind

Kyle. He's going to be your boss for the entire summer. Do you understand me?" Mom said with her voice low.

I nodded my head yes.

"Now, I want you to give your sisters a hug goodbye," she said.

"Aw, Momma, do I have to? It's not like I'm going to be leaving forever."

"Do it," my dad said.

My parents walked with Kyle out to the car. Dad had my fishing rod, my Winchester rifle, and my duffle bag, and mom was carrying two bags of extra food and snacks. Kyle was carrying the small red ice chest full of cold stuff.

I was left standing there in the living room to hug my three sisters goodbye. Tammy was the easiest to get along with, so I hugged her first. She had no idea where I was going.

"Where ya goin?" she asked, as I bent over to hug her.

"He's going to the swamps," Charlene cried.

Tammy shook her head back and forth as she started to cry. "No, no, no. Don't go there, Rye, don't you go," Tammy cried, wrapped her arms around my legs and held on to me like a drowning person to a raft as she looked up at Marie.

"I'm going away, but Cousin Kyle will be there to look after me."

"Don't go; it's a bad place," Tammy said with wide eyes, tears spilling over her face.

I knelt beside her, pulled my four-year-old sister close to me, and looked up at the culprits standing off to the side.

Marie had a twisted look on her face, and Charlene turned to the Barbie doll in her hands.

"No, it's not a bad place. What got ya so spooked?" I asked her softly. She was truly scared for me.

Tammy leaned into me and whispered in my right ear, "If ya go ther te rougarooooou gonna—gonna—he's gonna eat ya!" Tammy cried and held on tighter.

I stood up, and for the first time I could ever recall wanted to punch my older sister for scaring my four-year-old sister so badly.

"Marie said if I didn't do what she said, the rougrooo was gonna come and eat my toes while I'm sleeping," Tammy screamed at all of us as she ran from the room.

"Go, run off for the entire summer and leave us with all the work, you stinkin' pig," Marie said with a hateful glare in her eyes.

I knew my parents would have a cow if they heard us talking like this, but they were outside talking with Kyle next to his car now.

"I plan on doing just that, and it will be the two of you stinkin' like pigs after doin' all the work I've done for as long as I can remember. I hope you have as good a summer as I plan on having. I hope you both fall in the pig slop when you go to feed the pigs," I said with a chuckle.

"You just wait 'til I tell Momma what you just said," Charlene said, as she tried to walk in front of me. I stuck my leg in the way.

"You tell Momma, and I'll tell Dad how you and Marie have been smoking his cigarettes up in the barn.

"I'll tell Mom I caught you going through her purse last week." I said while looking at Marie. "I'll tell everyone how you, Charlene, have been stealing candy bars from the five and dime store on Second Street for more than a year. You must both be sick and out of your minds if you think I'm going to let you ruin my summer with Kyle. I'll tell Dad how you've both frightened his favorite child beyond nightmares."

Neither of them said a word.

"Let's not forget who the writer in this family is, and I can conjure up a story, better than the both of you combined."

"I hope you plan on bringing that retarded mutt with you. You'll be awfully sorry if you leave that thing here all by himself this summer," Marie said with a wicked little grin tugging at the corner of her lips.

"I wouldn't think of leaving Butch here with the likes of the two of you."

I was going to have the best time of my life despite my sisters.

"Well, you ready to go?" Kyle asked as he turned to look at me.

"I was born ready.

"Is it OK for Butch to come with us?"

"I don't see why not. You'll have to keep an eye on him twenty-four hours a day."

"Of course. He's my best friend. I'm gonna run to the barn and grab his dog food."

"It's already in the car, along with his dog bowls and a new leash," Dad said as he hugged my neck.

"Thanks, Dad."

I shoved Butch in the back seat, hugged my parents once again, and we drove off into the sunset.

21

"I can't believe we're finally going. I've been waiting for this moment to come."

"What do you mean you've been waiting for this moment to come? I just told you about it today," Kyle said, staring straight ahead into the oncoming night.

I found it hard to believe it was after 8:00 p.m. already.

Whoops, I had opened my mouth too soon.

"I sort of heard you talking about it to my parents when you came down to visit for Easter."

"You mean you were eavesdropping."

"Yeah, I guess that is the word for it. You're not mad at me, are ya?"

"No, I'm not mad. Where were you hiding?"

"I was hiding behind the couch."

"You sneaky little devil."

We both laughed.

"I knew you were there all along."

"How did you know?"

"There was either a fan behind the couch or it had to be you. Every time your father blew cigarette smoke my way, and it started to drift down, it would come back up slowly. When I got up to go tell your sisters hi, I saw two bare feet on the floor behind the couch. I find it hard to believe that you've kept it a secret from everyone else all this time."

"Everyone but Butch," I said.

"Are you thirsty? There are Cokes in the cooler in the trunk."

"Yeah, I'm thirsty."

The star-lit sky was forgotten beneath the black clouds quickly swallowing the night.

Lightning lit up the darkness, but it was only for a second, and the thunder rolled across the night skies. We hit the interstate bridge that went over the Atchafalaya Basin at sixty-five miles per hour.

Directly in front of us a small car hit something in the road and spun out of control. Kyle quickly pulled his car over to the side of the interstate.

We both sat there silently, helplessly watching the car as it flipped over three times at lightning speed before settling upside down.

Then it slid across the interstate like it was being pulled by some giant unseen hands-on invisible cables across the darkened highway, throwing metallic sparks into the ever-present darkness. Then a small fire broke out under the car and spread across the undercarriage like a lit fuse to a pile of dynamite.

22

Everything was happening in slow motion. A massive bolt of lightning crept through the night. The car stopped sliding about fifty feet in front of us. Then the engine caught fire.

Kyle took one quick look at me, before opening the door. "Don't you move from this car!"

"You must be crazy!" I cried, as Kyle ran to the burning car. I opened my door and stepped outside.

"God, please send someone down this road really fast!" I spoke to the night sky.

The clouds moved away, and the full moonlight set everything aglow.

I looked in the back seat at Butch; he was still asleep. I knew I should have stayed in the car, like I was told to, but if Kyle was going to go up in flames, then I was going to go with him.

I took off running toward the car, I didn't know how much help I would be, but I had to help.

I ran up to the passengers' side of the car. Kyle was pulling at the door to get this young girl out of the car. She couldn't have been older than five, but she was small like my sister Tammy. "*Somebody Help! Oh God, help me!*" The lady screamed from inside the car.

The fire was growing larger by the second.

Kyle got the little girl from the car. She was unconscious and limp like a ragdoll without stuffing. Her face and hair and clothes were covered in black soot.

"Ryan, I want you to bring her over behind my car, fast!"

I stood there for a second, holding the limp little girl in my arms.

"*Move it, Ryan!*" Kyle shouted at me as he reached back into the burning car to help the woman.

"Oh God, *help me!*" I heard the woman scream again.

I could barely see him through the smoke and fire. He was halfway inside the car.

I laid the limp girl on the ground behind Kyle's car and ran back to the burning car.

I didn't think twice about it, I just knew I had to help Kyle get away from there.

Kyle had the woman more than halfway freed from the car.

"My leg, my leg!" the woman shouted.

I was standing almost directly behind Kyle, knowing that all of us could be dead at any moment.

The fire seemed to be crawling all over the car, upside down across the hood. The flames engulfed the entire windshield, turning it to black glass.

"Ryan, Ryan, where are you?" Kyle shouted over his shoulder.

"I'm right behind you," I said.

The fire hissed, sucked at the windshield, then crept inside and melted the dash.

"Help me! I don't want to die in here. The fire is inside the car! Help me!" the woman screamed hysterically from behind the thick curtain of smoke and flames.

We both yanked the woman from the car.

"Run," Kyle shouted.

The car exploded at our backs.

23

"Ryan! Are you all right?" Kyle asked over his shoulder.

"Oh God, please let my baby live!" The woman cried as Kyle helped the lady to the ground next to her unconscious child.

The little girl lay there on the wet road as if she were in a coffin. The clouds had returned, and the rain fell softly on her face. I looked back at the car still on fire, throwing wet, eerie orange and red glows into the falling rain.

Kyle went right to work on the little girl. He lifted her arm to check for a pulse. It was clear to see from his expression that the little girl had no pulse.

I knelt on the road right beside Kyle and the little girl and her mother. As I looked down at her, her face swirled into my little sister's face.

The only medical thing I knew was CPR; Kyle had taught our entire family the life-saving procedure. He had gone to college to become a doctor.

I looked down again at the little girl. Her face was black and misty from the smoke from the car. I looked over at her mom who was saying the same little prayer over and over again.

"Please, Lord let my baby live; please let her live; please let her live," she prayed through her tears.

"Ryan, pay attention!" Kyle demanded, in a tone of voice I had never heard from him before.

He put his ear to the little girl's chest. "Ryan, do you remember when I taught you CPR?"

"Uh-huh."

I couldn't believe all of this was happening. Where were the police? Where was the ambulance?

"Snap out of it, young man; let's do this," Kyle said.

"I'll do the mouth-to-mouth; you do the compressions."

Kyle tilted her head to the side and ran his fingers through her mouth to do a sweep.

"Remember to count," Kyle said, as I put one hand on the other and placed them where Kyle pointed on her chest.

"No, here," he said as he moved my hands a little to the right.

"Not really hard; she's small, so be careful.

"Count," Kyle said.

"One, two, three, four, five," I counted.

Kyle pinched her nose and blew three steady breaths into her mouth.

"One, two, three, four, five," I counted again. Again Kyle blew into her lungs.

"What's your daughter's name?" Kyle asked the woman.

"Angel," the woman whispered, in between her prayers asking God to save her child's life.

The car was still burning through the rain, like a torch in the middle of the road.

Kyle blew into her lungs for the third time.

"*Again!*" Kyle shouted at me.

I started counting one more time.

"Come on Angel, breathe, *breathe!*" Kyle demanded.

She started choking and crying.

"She's going to make it," Kyle said.

The little girl looked into Kyle's eyes.

"Where's my mommy?" she cried.

"I'm right here baby. Mommy's right here."

Kyle handed her over to her mother. Both of them rocked in the misting rain. It seemed like hours since the car had lost control, flipped over, and caught fire. Then out of nowhere, as if they were waiting for us to do all the work, a lone police car pulled up behind us. The misty night sky streaked with red and blue lights from atop the police car.

"Ryan, I want you to go sit in the car while I talk to this officer." I got in the car without question. I looked over the back seat at Butch. He was fast asleep, snoring deeply on his back, all four legs sticking straight up in the air.

We saved two lives. It had all been less than twenty minutes.

The woman had thanked both of us and hugged our necks when we sat on the ground next to her.

I watched as the officer stood there talking to both for what seemed like a long time. He was writing things down on a metal clipboard.

24

"Why did you help them? You could have gotten both of us killed," I asked, as I started to shake, and tears burned behind my eyes.

"Because, Champ, that is what I went through so many years at college to do, to help save people's lives."

Kyle pulled the car over to the side of the interstate after we got around the burning car. He turned the interior light on so he could get a better look at me.

"I took one look at you back there, and knew I could not sit there and watch those people burn to death.

"I could not have lived with myself if those people died, and I could have done something to help them out."

"Let's get this one thing straight though. The next time I tell you to stay in the car, you had better do just that. Do you understand me?"

"I was not going to sit there and let you burn up," I said through tears I refused to let fall.

"Come here," Kyle said, as he pulled me into a big brotherly hug.

"Look at me," Kyle said taking my chin in the palm of his hand.

"I don't know what I would have done if you had been killed back there. Your parents would never have forgiven me if something happened to you. I know I would never have forgiven myself.

"Don't you know I love you like a brother?"

"I know that."

"But tell me honestly, doesn't it feel good to know we saved that woman and that little girl's life?"

"We both did it," I said, suddenly feeling ten feet tall.

"We sure did, didn't we?" Kyle said. "You're a real live hero."

"You're the hero," I said and stared out into the night.

We were both silent for the moment, lost in our own thoughts.

"No one will ever believe I did any of that."

"It doesn't matter what others believe; it matters what's true."

"Do you think sometime this summer, we could find out how to get a police report?"

"I'm sure it won't be hard, but why?"

"I told my teacher I would be writing about everything I'm doing this summer. If I had a police report, I think it would give others cause to believe what I'm writing is true."

"How old are you again?" Kyle asked.

"You know how old I am. I'm thirteen, today."

"I've got your final birthday gift on the houseboat."

"What is it?"

"You'll have to keep on guessing, Buddy."

"Come on, tell me."

"Nope."

"So how much farther do we have to go before we get to the place where we're meeting your friend?"

"About ten more minutes."

The rain had stopped, and some of the clouds parted, allowing the light of the moon to cast eerie glows all around us.

25

"It seems like we've been on this bridge forever. How long is this bridge anyway?"

"It's almost eighteen miles long."

"Well, Champ, we're almost there," Kyle said, as he took a sharp right turn.

For a second, I thought we were going to drive right off the bridge.

The Atchafalaya Basin was all around us. There was a huge open parking lot with other trucks and cars and empty boat trailers down under the bridge, and a road that seemed to be floating just above the water that went deeper into the backwoods of the Basin.

"Have you ever seen this houseboat?" I asked.

"Yes. Dennis was working on a huge project for his father at the lagoon that the houseboat is parked in. I was out here for almost a month during my last break at college."

"How will we find it in the dark? Are you sure we're not lost?"

"No. I've been in this area before. You see, we can't drive up to the houseboat. It is way out past where this road ends."

"*Stop!*" I shouted, as a huge alligator was crossing the road.

"Holy cow, look how big that thing is." Kyle was like a kid again, and as curious as I was.

"It can't get in the car, can it?" I asked as the alligator stopped.

It was like a deer caught in headlights; it wouldn't move.

"Why isn't it moving?" I asked.

It opened its mouth as if it wanted to bite the car.

"It's startled and confused as to what this car is in front of him. He sure is a big one."

"How big is that thing?" I asked in wonderment.

"Got to be a twelve-footer. It's one of the biggest I've ever seen."

"He could swallow me in one gulp," I said as I locked my door.

"He can't open the door, Ryan."

Suddenly Butch was in the front seat with his feet propped up on the dashboard, his nose pressed into the windshield looking down at the alligator in front of the car.

"What is that, Butch?" Kyle asked, as he rubbed Butch between the ears.

"That's a big kitty cat. Here kitty, kitty," I said.

Butch started barking at the glass, his entire body shaking back and forth, his tail swishing back and forth like a windshield wiper.

"Get the kitty," Kyle said to Butch.

Butch tried climbing onto the dashboard barking louder, licking at the windshield as if the glass weren't there at all. His back feet were in my chest as he lunged at the gator through the glass.

It was comically funny, and the absurdity and the laughter brought tears to my eyes 'til my sides ached.

Barking really loud now, the sound must have startled the gator.

It suddenly trotted across the road and vanished into the water at the edge of the road.

Kyle and I laughed.

26

"Are you sure we're not lost? What is this birthday gift you have for me?"

"No, we're not lost. This road will dead-end where we need to meet up with Dennis."

Kyle ignored the second part of the question.

We bounced off the paved road onto a gravel one.

Butch stirred in the back seat as we hit a pothole. The road came to a dead end, right into a very small parking lot. We parked right next to a beat-up old Ford pickup.

"That's Dennis's truck," Kyle said. "I want you to stick close to the car, and keep Butch on a tight leash, you got it? Let's not ever forget where you're at."

I looked around to be sure there wasn't another huge gator where we were parked.

I got out and stretched my short legs. The crickets were so loud you would have thought there were a million of them right where we stood.

Dennis's truck looked to be really worn out. The back end of the truck was held together by the little bit of rust that had not eaten all the way through.

"I hope the houseboat doesn't look as bad as his truck," I said as I let Butch out of the back seat and held on tightly to his leash. "What time is it?" I asked while walking to the other side of the car.

"It's almost midnight."

"Where is he? He was supposed to meet us here," Kyle said, as he walked over toward Dennis's truck.

"Then again, we're over an hour late." Kyle found a note under one of the windshield wipers.

"What does it say?" I asked.

"Kyle, I waited for you for over an hour. I figured you guys might have had car trouble or were just running late. Call me on the CB in my truck. It's set to the same station here on the houseboat. See you guys soon, Dennis."

Kyle opened the door to the truck and called him on the CB. "All right, Dennis said he should be here in about fifteen minutes."

The swampy waters seemed to be covered in a pale-yellow glare from the glow of the moonlight. Huge moss-covered cypress trees bolted upright from the swampy waters.

We got our things out of the car and placed them at the water's edge. Ten minutes later, Dennis drove up to the side of the dirt levee and drove the airboat right upon the ground.

Dennis stood about six feet two. His tall frame was very thin, too thin for someone so tall. He had jet-black hair, coal-black eyes, and a nose long and pointed. He had a pair of farmer brown coveralls on that were crudely cut just below the knees, and that was it, no shoes or shirt.

"I don't know about you guys, but I am dead tired," Dennis said. "I'm Dennis," he said as he reached out to shake my hand.

"Ryan, thanks for letting me hang out this summer. I hope it's OK that I brought my dog; this is Butch."

We placed our things in the front of the boat, and after several minutes of pleading I got Butch to get into the boat. He was not happy about it—not one bit. "Sorry, old boy. We gonna get in and out of boats all summer, you's just gonna have to get used to them."

27

Butch did everything but jump overboard. He was a nervous wreck. I sat down on the floor of the boat next to him and yanked my T-shirt away from my body and pulled him next to my skin. Then I yanked my shirt down over his head, holding him tightly to my chest, trying to calm him.

"It's OK, boy; it's OK," I whispered in his ear, and I rubbed his stomach. He calmed down and soon was dozing off.

"I'm afraid we're in for some bad weather," Dennis shouted at us over the roar of the engine.

Kyle stood next to Dennis staring straight into the darkness. Dennis had a hard hat on with two flashlights attached to either side of the hat, held firmly in place by duct tape.

Just up ahead the swamp split into four different sections. We took a sharp, sharp right turn, and then the swamp broke off into a wide bayou. Dennis threw the engine into high gear, and we took off like a rocket. I swear that half the boat was a foot above the water, just gliding on air, and I'm sure it was just that.

The night air felt good blowing in my face. The misty rain was all but forgotten. Butch started moaning, but he didn't move much.

For what seemed miles through the bayou, we were into the swamp again. Dennis cut the speed, and the boat lowered back into the water.

Clouds vanished overhead, and the full moon cast glossy glows across the surface of the swamps.

"Hey, Ryan," Dennis called to me.

"Yeah." I turned to look up at him.

"If it's not raining tomorrow, I'll teach you how to drive this thing."

"I'd love that. Thank ya." I wanted to drive this thing the moment I got on it. It was the coolest airboat I'd ever seen.

My first day at being a "swamp rat," and I loved every moment of it. I leaned over the edge of the boat to let my hand drag in the cool water.

Butch started moaning again.

"It's OK, boy, I'm right here; I'm right here," I whispered in his ear.

To the right was a small grassy levee, with one huge moss-covered cypress tree leaning out from the levee. Below the tree was a huge alligator. It lay there floating in the water watching us with big glowing red eyes. I was surprised it didn't run off from the roar of the engine. It opened its mouth really wide, as if to say, "You like my big teeth?"

Dennis cut the engine, and the airboat drifted slowly through the water. Just in front of us was another enormous cypress tree. Moss was dripping from every branch. It stood alone, bolting right up through the water. Just on the other side, hidden in the shadows, stood a small houseboat.

28

"Well, there she floats, boys; we're home."

"Old Lucy is her name," Dennis said, as we drifted up next to the huge floating dock that Old Lucy was anchored to.

"More like, Drowning Lucy," I whispered to Butch.

Forget houseboat; it was a floating piece of junk. It was a common run-of-the-mill shack, or better yet, an overgrown outhouse.

"Old Lucy has been floating in these here swamps for more than forty years now," Dennis said, as he jumped from the deck of the boat to the dock.

She looked more like a 140 years, I thought.

Dennis quickly tied the airboat to the dock and waited for us to get off.

"I know she needs some work, but she still floats."

Kyle and I were quiet for the moment.

I was in a state of shock.

Needs some work? Needs some work? He needed to sink it to the bottom of the swamp. At least the fish would have something to play in. This was one huge floating dock with two other boats, a small fishing boat and a pirogue tied to it.

"This has got to be a joke," I mumbled to myself. What little paint that clung to the houseboat seemed to be falling off. "It's kind of hard to see in the dark," I finally said.

"It doesn't look that bad, right, Champ?" Kyle said, as he picked up his duffel bag. Of course Kyle had been here before and stayed out here for weeks.

"Uh-huh," I said.

Four old-fashioned rockers sat at the front of the deck and three more sat at the back of Old Lucy. An old homemade barbecue pit sat just to the right of the rocking chairs. The roof of the houseboat was pretty much flat with a slight tilt at the back. There was a small wooden staircase that hugged a side wall of Old Lucy that went to the top of the roof.

I looked up at all the stars and the full moon and wondered if we were going to get any of that bad weather Dennis had talked about earlier.

29

The inside turned out to be a little better. There was a small eight-track radio boom box with a pile of eight-tracks stacked next to it sitting on one of the built-in shelves to the right of the door, next to stacks of novels and board games. The living room area was the largest room on the houseboat.

It was one large room with a curtain divider down the middle.

A small wooden plank bar table was attached to the wall, and three equally small folding wood chairs in what appeared to be the kitchen area. There was an old couch with no legs, and it sat on the floor next to the bookshelf, an old rocker next to that.

The tiny kitchen hugged one wall. A small propane cook stove, with two burners, sat on a small shelf just above a large red cooler.

On the other side of the divider were three sets of bunk beds built into the wall, and built-in shelves for clothes. It was sort of like our tree-house back at the farm, but floating.

The coolest thing was the door. I kept looking at it. It was an old, heavy, wooden door, with a helm, "the ship's wheel," attached to the inside of the door; there were actually two of them, one on each side of the door.

"That's right guys, I failed to mention that there is no electric out here. Of course Kyle knew this, but failed to tell you, Ryan, I take it. It's like summer camp but in the middle of the largest swamp in the United States. I don't know about you guys, but I am hitting the sack."

"If there's no electricity, how is this old fan working, and what about the eight-track radio?"

"I've got two car batteries in a hidden shelf under the eight-track radio. They are wired to a power-strip cord. It's enough to power the fan and the radio. But we only use the fan at night. We use the eight-track radio when we are bored with the silence, or to tune in to bad weather."

Dennis climbed up into one of the top bunks. "I see you staring at the helm on the door. They were pulled from sunken pirate ships in the Gulf of Mexico, as well as the door. My grandfather fashioned the locking system when he and my father first built this houseboat. It's quite simple really; just turn the helm to your left when you're inside and it moves the lock to the left, and right to close. It is the same as the outside, but in the opposite direction, of course. When you are the last one inside, or the last one to close the door, always slide the other steel latch at the top of the door to keep the door locked. We don't want no gators in here." Dennis laughed.

I looked at one of the shelves to stack clothes on. There were more than enough shelves to sort our clothes out nice and neat, but we were all tired.

I left my duffle bag on the floor, yawned, and walked toward the bottom bunk on the right. "Is it all right if Butch sleeps with me?" I asked Dennis, as I climbed into the bed.

"As long as you know that if he craps in here, you clean it up."

"He won't; he's well trained. We're gonna go back outside for a few minutes," I said to Kyle.

I took another look at my home for the entire summer under the light of a full moon. I could be back at the farm with my three sisters and all the farm work, yuck. The houseboat was not so bad looking after all.

While sitting there in one of the old rockers, I fell in love with Old Lucy.

30

I bolted upright from the sound of thunder rolling over my head. The stars and moonlight had vanished.

The thunder rolled long and deep, and another bolt of lightning struck the cypress in front of the houseboat. An ear-shattering crack tore through the night, and the tree crashed down onto the houseboat.

I reached for Butch's collar, but he was gone.

The impact of the tree's fall threw me to the floor.

"No!" I screamed.

"Kyle! Dennis!" I shouted as I got to my feet.

There was no answer.

I more than stared in disbelief at the houseboat. I was barely four feet two, and the rooftop of the houseboat was at eye level to me.

"Kyle! Dennis!" I yelled at the top of my lungs.

Still there was no answer.

What remained of the houseboat started to sink. The back end of the houseboat where the tree had rolled started to go down. It was as if the tree underneath was pulling it down. The water was gushing over the deck from every side. Within seconds I was knee deep in water.

"Butch! Kyle! Dennis!" I screamed in fear.

There was no way for me to get inside to check on them.

"Oh, God, help me!" I yelled into the night.

It was either get on the dock or drown, though the dock seemed to be going under as well.

I stood there in disbelief as the houseboat vanished from sight. Tears stung my eyes, and I was shaking uncontrollably.

31

I woke up to feel Butch's tongue slithering across my forehead.
Wait a minute.

I looked straight ahead. The houseboat was in front of me. It had all been a nightmare.

The houseboat stood in all her glory. I got up from the rocking chair I had fallen asleep in and hugged the wall of the houseboat.

"Old Lucy, I love you," I said.

"I take back everything I said or thought about you."

"Come on, old boy, let's go inside."

Both Kyle and Dennis were sound asleep in their bunks.

"Kyle," I whispered as I nudged him on the shoulder.

He rubbed his eyes and yawned.

"Yeah, what is it, Champ?"

"Thanks for bringing me out here," I said, climbing in the bunk I'd chosen for the summer.

Butch climbed in behind me, turned around in four circles until his comfortable spot found him, and he fell down, all four legs sticking up in the air as he pressed his body into my lower backside. Within moments he was fast asleep.

"Get some sleep. Things will look a lot better tomorrow."

I knew my life of freedom for the summer would look a lot better in the next few days.

I woke to the smell of fresh coffee.

Dennis was cooking breakfast.

"It sure smells good," Kyle said, jumping down from his bunk in his worn-out jeans and his stained T-shirt.

"Where's the bathroom?" I asked, looking around the houseboat for a door that led to a toilet.

"Sorry, Buddy, I guess your cousin forgot to tell you, we ain't got no bathroom."

"How can there be no bathroom?"

"There's a pot there under your bunk."

"Are you serious?"

It was a white pot with a handle and a heavy white plastic lid. I knew this well. My grandmother still had one in her house, even though it was 1977. A pochum is what my grandma called it. You would use it (the lid held in the smell), and you would haul it out to the outhouse.

"Welcome to the swamps, Champ," Kyle said, as he pulled the curtain across the rod so I could have some privacy.

Afterward, I sat down to eggs and bacon and a cup of hot black coffee. The coffee was strong and nasty, but after a couple swallows it wasn't so bad.

"Where's Kyle?" I asked, noticing he wasn't there.

"He took Butch outside. You drink coffee, right?"

"Yes. I like coffee. Dad lets me have some before the farm work, and that's early."

"After you finish breakfast, I'll show you where we empty the pot."

"Can you move this houseboat?" I asked, as I drank the last of my coffee.

"Sure can. Why do you ask?"

"Can we move it?"

"Why do you want to move it?"

"I had this horrible nightmare last night."

"Go on, I'm listening," Dennis said; he sat in the chair next to me.

He was all ears as I told him about the twisted nightmare I had about Old Lucy sinking.

"I wouldn't worry about it too much. It looks like the bad weather has passed us by. You can never trust the weathermen.

"In your dream, you said a huge cypress crashed onto Old Lucy. You must have seen it wrong. The only cypress is way out to the left. We're pretty much out in the open. The mind plays tricks out here in the middle of the swamp."

32

"There's all kinds of thangs in t'is swamp t'at could kill ya—snakes, gators, spiders, even some of the folks that live in this swamp," Dennis said. He started a new pot of coffee and spoke in a deep southern voice that went on and off like a light switch.

"People live back here?" I asked.

Kyle and Butch walked back in as Dennis kept talking.

"Of course they do; for more than one hundred years, people have lived in these swamps. If ya pass one of them there houses out here, do not go on their property. They would just as soon as kill you as say 'hi' to ya. They are very private out here, and they don't take lightly to strangers. So that rule must always stay in your head. Don't bother other folks you may run into out here. If they want to speak, however, don't ever be rude."

"I want you to keep this with you at all times." Dennis handed me a small compass attached to a piece of leather rope.

"Have you ever used one of these?"

"Yeah, my dad has one."

"OK, let's go outside on the deck for a moment."

We all walked out the door to the deck. I looked toward the huge cypress. Sure enough, the tree lurked way out to the left.

"I want you to look completely around you. Do ya have any idea where we are?" Dennis asked.

"No, but if I were to guess, I would say we are in the middle of a lagoon."

"Very good, Sport. That means there is only one way in and one way out."

"Can you tell me which direction that is?"

"South," I said, pointing in the direction of the huge path on the water and looking down at the compass.

"There are hundreds of these little lagoons in this swamp, though the one we're in is far from little." Dennis placed one hand on my shoulder and pointed beyond the path that vanished through the trees.

"If the compass was not on your neck, do you think you could find your way back here?"

I looked around, and spotted a yellow flag attached to one of the top branches in the huge cypress to the left of Old Lucy.

"Very good," Dennis said as he saw me looking up at the flag.

"That flag has saved me a lot, but you can get lost very quickly out there."

"You're going to stick with me and your cousin for a few weeks, if not more than half the summer. Every time you make a turn onto another path in this swamp, you write it down, and the direction you just came from. If you keep track of the direction of each turn, you should be OK. Should you decide you's bigger than yer thirteen-year-old britches, and decide to leave this lagoon without me, your cousin or my other friend from college who will be joining us for the summer …" I kept looking around., "hey, hey, eyes up here," Dennis said, snapping his fingers with a loud pop. "If you decide to leave this lagoon alone, I will put you on the fast boat home, you got me?"

"I got ya."

"Don't play me, kid. I want ya to have fun out here, but alone can get you into serious trouble, or dead. Quickly dead—do we understand each other?"

I nodded my head.

"If you are out there on one of these boats by yourself on an adventure, you will be back here in this area an hour before the sun starts to fall. Ya got all that? Eyes on yer dog at all times, or something could eat him easily, and always have a gun in the boat."

"Yeah, I got it."

"I am dead serious, if you are not here an hour before the sun sets, and we have to go out there and look for you, and we find you, and you're not harmed at all, then I will have Kyle bring you back to your family. I'm not being mean; I just want you to have fun but not get hurt out there."

"He's got it. I've pounded the same thing into his head the entire drive to where you picked us up last night," Kyle said, looking around.

"When do we leave to go explore?" I said, looking at the surroundings again.

"As soon as we pack some sandwiches and cold drinks for lunch," Kyle said. I yanked a blanket from one of the beds, so Butch wouldn't burn himself on the bottom of the boat in this heat.

33

I watched everything Dennis did as he started the engine. There was a key and a button, and then the engine roared to life. We slowly left the dock, eased out of the lagoon area, and picked up speed down the small bayou at the end of the lagoon.

"All right, Sport," Dennis said, looking at me.

"Come here, and I'll teach you how to drive this thing."

There was a small step stool just left of the seat. It was set up like a barber's chair. There was a small metal footpad in front of the seat. The control bars were just left and right to the footpad and on it three pieces of duct tape in a row going toward the front of the boat with bold lettering. The first one at the driver's feet said, "Okay." The second piece of tape said, "Yeehaw." and the third toward the front of the boat said, "Hang on!)"

"Ya see the tape with the words written on the footpad in front of you?" Dennis asked, his back to me.

"Yes."

"And what zone are you not to go in?"

"Hang on!"

"You get an A-plus. You could flip this boat easily, and who would be the first in the water, and possibly eaten by a gator? Yes, that would be Butch. Just recall when you are driving this or any other boat out here, you are responsible for the lives within that boat. Now, I want you to show me where the logbook is, and what you think you should do if we turn right, here."

I looked around, and found a metal clipboard underneath the seat, attached to two strip magnets, with a pen on a string attached to the clipboard and an old tablet within the metal covers.

I held the compass out in front of me. We were pointed south. I turned it to the right, and we would have gone west.

I looked down at the clipboard and saw how simple it was. R. stood for right, L. stood for left, and N.S.E.W., stood for the directions.

I wrote down "R. W."

"You get an A plus." Dennis said to Kyle as he looked at the clipboard. "You're going to be a full-bred 'swamp rat' by the end of the week."

I looked over at Butch who was fast becoming easy with the boat. He was lying on his back, all four legs in the air, his tail slapping the boat's floor like a drummer beating a drum. He was happy as I was to be here.

"If you forget about your compass on your neck, look at the clipboard. There is a small compass in the right-hand corner. The same type of clipboard setup is on the other two lager boats as well."

"The controls are easy. There're two control bars in front of you. The one on the right acts like the gas pedal in a car. Push it forward and we move. Push it all the way, and we fly through the air like my grandmother on a broomstick. But you have to go at it slow. Don't you shove it forward, or you could easily flip this boat and kill us all. The bar on your left controls the turns."

"You know why they call this an airboat, don't you?"

"No."

"At full speed, this boat is gliding on air right above the water, and I don't want you to get to that point until the end of the summer. You got it?"

"Yes."

"Can you tell me when the first airboat was invented, and by whom?"

"I know the answer."

"You do, do you?" Kyle asked, turning to look at me.

"I secretly did some research on things, when I found out I was going to be here for the summer. I was hoping for this moment right here," I said looking down at them from my captain's chair. "The person to invent the airboat, also known as a planeboat, was Alexander Graham Bell, way back in 1905."

"Very good, Sport, now look behind you." Dennis placed his hand firmly on my hand on the control bar.

"Notice the rudders on the back of the fan? Right to left, east to west. Pretty simple."

"We're going to take a right here and take it straight to the beaches that are about five miles down this bayou. There'll be no other turns."

"Let's go," Dennis said, moving to the front of the boat, sitting on the blanket next to Butch, who accepted the free belly rubs offered.

Kyle winked at me and threw me a baseball cap he yanked out of a small army duffle bag.

I caught it and put it on.

"Let's go," Kyle said with both thumbs up while wiping the sweat from his forehead. The humidity was sweltering.

I started the engine, grabbed hold of the control bars, turned the rudders to the right, pushed forward on the gas bar, and we flew through the air. I kept the bar halfway forward and kept it under control.

It was simple.

It was easy.

It was the coolest feeling in the world.

34

The scenery constantly changed, from huge trees, to small pines, to smaller bushes. Everywhere you looked the gators remained, floating there near the shoreline like logs, hungry logs, looking for something to eat.

The swamp area vanished, as the river area that Dennis talked about earlier appeared in front of us.

It was one hot day, and I couldn't wait 'til we reached the swimming spot. There were times when I thought I should have been born a fish, as much as I liked the water.

"There's the spot," Dennis shouted over the roar of the engine.

"I've been coming here since I was younger than you," Dennis said as we drifted onto the sand. There were quite a few trees jutting over the water and sandy beach area, plenty of shady spots, which was nice. There were a few fallen trees on both sides of the small river area, and I kept looking to see which one of them might have feet.

I didn't see any gators around. That was a plus. Dennis and Kyle jumped in the water and swam out to the middle. I stood there on the shore, Butch next to me.

"How do you know there aren't gators hiding someplace waiting to eat you?" I asked.

"You don't; that's half the fun of swimming out here."

"Are you crazy?"

"Gators aren't usually down this way. I come here every summer. I've not run into one yet in this area."

I got in the water as Butch found a shady spot to lie in. He was a happy camper. It was getting dark by the time we got back on the airboat.

It was a race against time to get back to Old Lucy before the sun vanished.

The cool air felt good on my face as Dennis threw the boat into "Hang on!" and we went flying.

Moss-covered cypress trees appeared on both sides of the bayou.

Floating gators, lurking under trees, stared with wide eyes.

Slithering snakes across the top of the water slid past the boat.

A big spider crawled over the edge of the boat straight toward my lap. I got closer to it and flicked my finger at it. It went flying over backward back into the water.

35

It seemed all the creatures of the night were running their mouths. The crickets were the loudest of them all. Next were the bullfrogs. An owl hooted somewhere nearby, and the sound of some wild creature barked.

"There are dogs that live out here?" I asked, turning to look at Dennis.

"There are wild dogs everywhere. But look there next to you; that looks like a dog to me."

I looked down at Butch.

We all stepped from the airboat to the dock and were a bit shocked when we took a closer look at Old Lucy.

She was leaning badly to the right. She seemed to be sinking to her slow and timely death.

We had to move fast, or the houseboat was a goner.

Within minutes the houseboat would be at the bottom of the swamps, and I would be on my way back to the farm.

"We have to do something quick!" I said looking at Dennis.

"All right you guys, let's not panic. This has happened to Old Lucy before, when I was fifteen."

The sky streaked in brilliant shades of reds, oranges, and dark blue, but we were losing the sunlight as fast as we were losing Old Lucy.

"Kyle, I want you to drive the airboat around to the back of the houseboat. We'll have to turn Old Lucy completely around and anchor the sinking side to the dock. Trust me, she won't sink."

"Ryan, I want you to get in the other boat and drive it to the back side of Old Lucy as well, side by side with Kyle. Give me a moment to untie her from the dock on the now-sinking side. Butch can stay on the dock with me."

"Stay in line. *Let's do this!*" Dennis shouted over the roar of the engines, as we got into place.

The sinking end had dropped a few more inches deeper into the water. Dennis told Butch not to move, and Butch didn't budge an inch, which I found a little freaky. He was my dog and didn't listen to me half as well.

Dennis jumped from the dock, across the deck of Old Lucy, to the back of the airboat Kyle was on. Both tied the sinking end to the metal frame that held up the captain's seat. Dennis jumped back on the deck and ran to the front of Old Lucy, picked up the other heavy, soaking rope that had been untied moments ago and started dragging the rope slowly.

Kyle and I started pushing our boats forward, slowly turning the houseboat around.

I didn't see how it was possible, but the boat started to slowly turn around, and we slowly got the sinking side up against the dock. I glanced under the houseboat to notice she was held up by old metal drums, just like the ones Momma used to burn trash in back on the farm.

Kyle got out of the airboat and helped Dennis tie two of the ropes of Old Lucy to the edge of the dock.

I got out of the fishing boat and stood next to Kyle.

Dennis repositioned the airboat once more and threw the other two ropes over the dock. The airboat started to drive forward slowly, which pulled the sinking end up and out of the water.

We tightened the ropes at both ends of the dock really tight.

Dennis yelled at both of us, pointing toward the extra rope lying up against the back of the houseboat. We tied those into knots quickly, keeping Old Lucy afloat.

I heard a splash.

"Butch, you get back here right now!" I screamed at him.

"He can swim pretty good," Kyle said breathing heavy after all we had done.

"He hates the water," I said.

"What's he doing?" Dennis asked.

"Go, go, go get him," Kyle said.

"There's an alligator swimming right toward him!" I screamed at Dennis.

36

Dennis was in the driver's seat of the airboat. The engine roared to life. He sped out toward the gator, which vanished from sight the minute the engine started. He shoved the boat between the spot where the gator had been and where Butch was still swimming. He cut the engine, jumped from the driver's chair, reached over and yanked Butch into the boat and came back to the dock.

I kept looking in all directions to see where the alligator had gone.

It was nowhere to be seen.

I slipped my hand under Butch's collar and had him sit next to me on the dock.

I kept checking him to see if he was OK.

"Let that be a lesson. You need to keep an eye on him at all times," Dennis said.

"I told you there are things in this swamp that could easily kill you."

"So, Sport, it is your turn to cook dinner tonight."

"Find something in the ice chest and get to it."

"We'll have a nice barbecue out here by the end of the week, after we run to Baton Rouge for supplies and a grocery run."

"Take Butch inside, so Kyle and I can look at this boat once more."

"Thanks for saving Butch," I said hauling him across the dock to the deck of the houseboat.

"It's not a problem. I like that dog."

"We have to make sure these knots are good and tight," I heard Dennis say to Kyle.

I looked in the cabinets to find something to cook. Hot dogs, potato chips, and macaroni and cheese sounded good enough and easy enough. I found a can of evaporated milk and made do. I had it all whipped up in twenty minutes and had three plates loaded with food the minute the guys stepped in the living area.

I kept looking over at Butch, who sat beside Dennis as if they had suddenly become best friends. "How did you do that earlier?" I asked Dennis, digging into my macaroni and cheese.

"Do what?" Dennis asked.

"How did you make Butch listen to you so easily?"

"I have a way with most animals. I really like this dog, but you have to keep a closer eye on him. I won't always be there to protect him."

"Protect him from what?" I asked.

"You seriously need to ask, after he just almost got eaten in front of you."

We all turned to look at Butch, who tilted his head to the right to sit there and listen to us as if he knew for a fact that we were talking about him.

"I believe the boat will hold until we can get her fixed," Dennis said, winking at Butch. "Getting Old Lucy fixed is an easy thing; it's just removing all rusted barrels that are leaking and replacing them with new ones.

"You did a good job at cooking," said Kyle.

"Thanks."

When we were all done, I did the dishes without question.

"Kyle, are ya up for a game of chess?" Dennis asked.

"As long as you don't cry if I win," Kyle said.

"You wish," Dennis laughed.

"So, Champ, you having a good vacation so far?"

"The best ever; thanks for bringing me out here."

"You're welcome; your birthday gift is on the bed."

It was an old typewriter, with new reel-to-reel ribbons, pens and paper, a new journal, a dozen ringed tablets with multi-colored cardboard covers, and an instructional booklet on how to teach yourself how to type.

I looked up.

Kyle and Dennis were standing there looking at me.

"Thank you. You know Mom would have a fit if she saw all this stuff you're giving me."

"You're welcome."

"I want you to take in everything you can this summer.

"Haul the journal or tablets everywhere with you, and day-by-day type something.

"I know how you are always telling stories. You need to start writing them down, and then start typing. Thousands of people every day teach themselves to type, to play the guitar, play the piano, drive a car, or drive a boat. You want it bad enough, it'll come super easy; you got to practice, practice, practice," Kyle said to me.

37

Two hours had passed, and I had read the entire booklet on teaching you how to type.

I managed to write and fill up six pages in my new journal about what had taken place today alone.

"Tomorrow we will haul Old Lucy to the shore to work on the repairs. I think we'll just keep her tied up to the shore for a while."

"I'm turning in for the night," Dennis said as he stretched his long legs, and climbed up in his bunk as Butch and I went outside.

I had Butch on his leash. He was not about to go in the swamp this late.

"I'm going to bed for the night," Kyle said quietly.

"What time is it anyway?" I asked.

"It's almost midnight," Kyle said with his hand on the door. "Don't stay up too late."

"I won't."

I jumped up and down on the deck for a moment to see if Old Lucy could stand the pressure. She didn't budge an inch. I sat back in one of the old rockers next to Butch.

There seemed to be a billion lightning bugs out floating all around the houseboat. Looked like a bunch of sparkling Christmas lights over the water. The little lights cast glows on the surface of the water.

Looking up at all the stars, it was so fantastically cool. I stood there for a while in awe of it all.

"Come on, old boy, let's turn in."

He jumped down from the chair he was sitting in as if he were one hundred years old, walking slowly across the deck, as if he had been hard at work all day.

I laughed at the thought. Butch wouldn't know a hard day's work if it fell on him like a ton of bricks.

We walked back to the door. I placed my hand on the helm and turned it to the right.

I never gave a thought to the red eyes at the shore that stared at Butch as I closed the door tight.

38

I woke up to the smell of Butch's breath in my face.

"What's the problem, Butch?" I asked.

The sun was shining through the tattered curtains.

I found it hard to believe it was morning already. It seemed as though I had just closed my eyes.

Butch kept barking, looking out over the edge of the bed.

"Can't you shut him up," Dennis said, flipping over in his bunk to face the wall.

I pulled myself to a sitting position and looked out over the bed to see what Butch was barking at.

The entire floor was under water. The water was almost up to the edge of the bed I was on. My heart slammed in my chest.

A diamondback water snake was floating on the water next to the small Igloo cooler in the kitchen area. Its back was to me, but it was slowly turning around.

"*Oh my God!*" I shouted.

"Get up, you guys! We're sinking!"

Butch started whining like a scared child.

"*Get up now! I'm not joking!*" I screamed at both of them. I pounded my fist on the bottom of the bunk above my bed.

"This shack is going under, and there is a snake in here swimming toward Butch!" I quickly made my way to the top bunk that Kyle was on.

I threw the pillow down at the snake, and it changed directions and swam under the bottom bunk that Dennis was on.

"Where's the snake?" Kyle asked me.

"It's under the bottom bunk where Dennis is."

Dennis sat up casually, as if it were a normal thing to have water and a huge snake inside the houseboat.

The water was rising fast.

All the metal drums under the houseboat must have sprung leaks.

The houseboat was not leaning either to the right or the left.

We were going straight down to the soggy bottom.

"*Get Butch up here!*" I begged as my dog started to whimper.

Dennis got down in the water.

He handed Butch to me.

"Thanks," was all I could say.

"There's a snake down there," said Kyle.

"We've got to get out of here, or we're going to drown in this house-boat," said Dennis.

"What about the snake?" I asked, as Dennis waded through the water into the kitchen area.

"Snakes are normally scared of people. The fact he didn't come out from under the bed when I jumped into the water proves that."

"I'm sure it is trying to get back outside," said Kyle.

"I would like to know how it got in here to begin with." My heart was pounding in my chest.

Kyle and I watched as Dennis kept trying to edge the snake out from under the bed with a frogging net he got from a hook on the wall by the door in the living room.

It did just that, swam out into the middle of the room.

Dennis caught it by the head with his right hand and quickly pulled it to him, while yanking the pillowcase on my bed from the pillow with his left hand, and in one swift movement, he shoved the head of the snake into the pillowcase, gently shoved the entire snake inside and quickly knotted the end of the pillowcase and sat it on the table where we had eaten dinner last night. "You's a big sucka ain't ya? Four, five feet easily," he said to the snake as he patted the pillowcase.

"Wow!" is all I could say.

I had a whole new respect for Dennis after what he just did, which was downright stupid crazy.

"We've got to get out of this houseboat." Dennis said, looking up at both of us.

"All your writing stuff is about to be under water, so you better get down here and throw it up on the top bunk," Dennis said, hauling one of the chairs from the living area over to the bottom of the window next to the bunk beds.

"The trick to having a blast, and surviving out here in theses swamps, is to respect that which has the power to kill ya or scare ya half to death. Ain't that right, Buddy?" Dennis whispered to the snake in the pillowcase.

Kyle and I looked at one another. There was more to Dennis than met the eye. That was crazy what he just did.

Dennis was a Lord of the Swamp.

39

"How deep is the water under this boat anyhow?" Kyle asked. "Twelve feet, maybe a little deeper at the center of the lagoon," Dennis said, climbing up on the chair.

He shoved the window open and pushed the screen out.

The water was still rising fast.

"We're sinking all right," Dennis said looking out the window.

How bright could one be? I laughed in my head.

"The deck is completely under water."

"That's funny," Dennis said, scratching the back of his head.

"What's funny?" Kyle asked.

"The ropes must have come untied from Old Lucy. A slight problem has just come up, come up out of the water that is; nope two of them," Dennis said.

"Two, what?" Kyle asked.

"Two alligators," said Dennis, as if it were a normal everyday occurrence to be in a sinking boat and have a couple gators there to catch you if you should go under.

I was writing all this in my mind so I could write it down in my journal, hoping we didn't sink or become breakfast for some gators.

I looked down at Butch who sat there with his tongue hanging out, wondering who knew what.

Kyle stood on the floor handing me the sheets and pillowcases and covers from the bottom bunks, and I shoved them in the corner of the top bed, along with all my writing stuff.

Dennis got down from the chair and went back into the living area to grab his father's shotgun.

He jumped back on the chair, cocked the shotgun, and fired out the window twice.

"Let's go before they come back. I want Kyle to go first. Ryan second, then Butch."

"Hurry, you guys, before they come back," Dennis said.

I handed Butch back down to Dennis, as Kyle crawled out the window.

"How are we going to save this houseboat?" I asked.

He cupped his hands, and I stepped into them as he pushed me up to the open window.

"I'll tell you when we get out."

For the moment Old Lucy had steadied herself. It was like she refused to sink another inch. "Don't you give up, old girl," I said to Old Lucy.

Just as Dennis was climbing out of the window, the two alligators appeared out of nowhere.

"Get back in! Get back in!" Kyle shouted.

But Dennis didn't budge.

He was midway in and midway out of the window, as Kyle, Butch, and I stood at the edge of the floating dock that Old Lucy had been anchored to.

We watched both the alligators closely. Then suddenly they vanished stealthily, as if they had never been there to begin with. No air bubbles, no water disturbance, just complete silence.

40

Another airboat came flying into the lagoon area, which surely must have scared any other gators farther away from wherever they may have been hiding.

Dennis jumped into the water, and Kyle and I helped him onto the dock.

The airboat did a full circle around the dock and Old Lucy sinking.

The driver of the boat cut the engine off. Two other guys were on the boat beside the driver.

They all looked to be Kyle and Dennis's age.

"Dennis, I thought that was you," the tall blond-haired guy said as he jumped from his boat to the dock.

"Hey, Greg," Kyle said to the short redheaded guy.

"Hey, Jimmy," Dennis said to the tall blond guy. "Man, I'm glad to see you guys. We need a hand before Old Lucy sinks to the bottom."

We all stood at the edge of the dock looking down at Old Lucy, who seemed to be screaming for help.

I stood there feeling bad, seeing the houseboat sinking like it was. She was drowning, and if she went completely under, I would be going home two days into my trip.

She dropped another six inches at least almost in the snap of a finger, and we all stood there helplessly looking at her gasping to stay afloat.

"I'm surprised Old Lucy has lived this long," Jimmy said.

"We've got to do something quick," Greg said, scratching his chin.

"We can tie two of the ropes to the back of your airboat and two to mine, then tie the knots to the front of Old Lucy's undercarriage," Dennis said to Jimmy.

"If we hurry, we should be able to drag her quite a bit up shore." The plan had been set, and all four ropes were untied from the floating dock. Kyle, Greg, and Jimmy started retying the ropes to the back of the airboats.

"The plan sounds good, but the deal is, who's going to be the one to go under the water and tie the ropes to Old Lucy?" said Jimmy.

"I will; I know right where the anchor bars are, and besides, my father would kill me if he knew I stood by and watched her sink," Dennis said.

"Someone else will have to go with you; she'll sink before you can even get two of the ropes tied," Jimmy said. He had a point.

"I'll go," Kyle said. Now that was a stupid choice, I thought.

"I want you to listen to Jimmy," Kyle said as he looked me in the eyes.

I just shook my head yes, but I wanted to shout at him not to go down there. Those gators could eat them both.

"Don't worry; things will turn out. The noise from the engines of the airboats will keep the gators away," Dennis said and got ready to jump.

Everything else happened as quickly as a gator snapping his jaw.

Greg jumped on Dennis's boat.

Me, Butch, and Jimmy jumped on his boat, and the engines were on high gear. Butch had grown used to the boats; he found a spot to sit and watch the action unfold.

Dennis walked across both boats to the far side, grabbed a rope, and dove under the water.

Kyle did the same on the boat I was standing on, Butch at my side.

We watched the air bubbles made by Dennis and Kyle rise to the surface.

Their bodies vanished completely from sight beneath the green murky waters. There was a violent tug on one of the ropes and the houseboat sank about two inches farther into the swamp.

It didn't seem possible to save the houseboat at all.

The other two ropes would have to be tied quickly, or she was a goner for sure.

It seemed like they were under water for way too long. I didn't see how they could hold their breath that long.

I looked over at Greg and Jimmy who stood on the back of the boats looking down. They looked just as worried as I was.

Even Butch started to whine when Kyle didn't come back up.

"Come on guys," the tall black-headed guy said, as he stood next to me. Both of their heads popped up at the same time. They took two deep breaths, grabbed the other ropes, and went back under again. Within a minute, both of them were back up and getting into the boats.

Dennis yelled at the top of his lungs for them to "punch it."

41

Our eyes were glued to Old Lucy. The boats weren't moving at all, it seemed.

The engines were running full speed.

The weight of the houseboat under the water was pulling heavy on the back of the airboats, and the front of both the airboats rose into the air.

It was a tug of war between the airboats, the drowning houseboat, and the excess swampy lagoon water that clawed at the drowning houseboat.

We got closer and closer to the shore, slowly but surely dragging Old Lucy from her untimely death. As we did, Old Lucy started to rise more and more, like an old pirate ship rising from the dead. The nose of both airboats rose higher and higher in the air, and we drug Old Lucy back from her sinking grave toward the shore.

There was a good stretch of land from the shore to the back. Both engines were gunned, and the airboats kept going.

The engine on Dennis's airboat began to blow smoke, sending a white fog backward.

Greg looked over at Dennis.

"Go, go!" Dennis shouted with both thumbs held high, stabbing the air with his fingers pointed toward a thicket of trees and shrubs at the way back of the shore.

Both airboats ran right up on the land, dragging Old Lucy through the smoke like that pirate ship drifting through a foggy morning.

Old Lucy had indeed come back from the dead. We could see underneath the entire houseboat.

I counted eight huge metal drums on each side. It looked like four on each side had rusted through and was crushed beyond repair.

"It doesn't look all that bad," Kyle said, and I thought maybe he was crazy.

"We'll have to make a trip to Baton Rouge so we can borrow some cash from dear old Dad. He's been expecting rust for a while now. Sport, you can call your folks from my parents' house. Just don't tell them about Old Lucy, unless you want to go home before the real fun begins."

We packed a few things that did not get water-damaged and jumped in the small fishing boat. Jimmy and Craig had vanished as quickly as they had appeared.

We drove the boat to the levee where Dennis's truck was parked.

I expected Dennis's truck wouldn't start, the way things were going, but she started up easily and purred like a kitten.

42

The main roads into Baton Rouge were bumper-to-bumper cars, trucks, and eighteen-wheelers.

Dennis's parents lived on the other side of Baton Rouge, so we had to drive straight through downtown to get there.

We bypassed the Mississippi River, and my eyes were glued to the huge ships that were jam-packed along the river's edge.

"So, Sport, are you having fun?" Dennis asked, as we stopped at a red light.

"The most," I said, continuing to look out the window.

It was the start of summer, a summer that would be etched into my memory for a lifetime.

"Be sure you don't let on that Old Lucy sank today," Dennis said, and we stopped at another traffic light.

Finally we pulled up to Dennis's parents' house.

It was easy to see his father knew we'd be coming. He had a long flatbed trailer in the front drive, with twelve brand new silver drums, ten gallons of paint, buckets of brushes, rollers, ropes, sheets of beadboard, cans of gasoline, and a ton of other supplies and boxes of food.

"Son, I've been meaning to fix Old Lucy up this summer, but I'll never get around to it."

"I've had these drums ordered for the past couple of months. Being as they're three of you out there, I expect all the work to be done before she springs a leak and sinks," Dennis's father said to us all hanging around the huge porch.

Too late, I wanted to shout.

"You must be Ryan," Dennis's mother said, coming up to me and hugging me as if she'd known me my entire life.

"Yes, ma'am."

"So, Ryan, what do you think of Old Lucy?" Dennis's father asked, shaking my hand.

"She's cool; needs a bit of paint though."

"Have you painted a house before? You look like a hard-working young man. I've heard you live on a farm. It's an amazing thing what paint can do for any old wreck. I've ten gallons of it sitting on that flatbed trailer out there with all the other supplies."

"It's a very small farm. I helped my dad paint our house last year."

"Will you make sure she gets properly painted?"

"I can't trust a paint brush in the hands of these two older goons you have to live with for the summer." Dennis's father winked at me, placing a strong hand on my shoulder.

"Yes, sir, I'll paint her up good."

"Kyle here talks about you a lot. He tells me you have a lazy dog?"

We all stepped off the porch.

"Yes, sir, he's in the back of the truck."

Sure enough, Butch was sleeping on his back, all four legs sticking straight up in the air in the back of the truck with the old blanket kept in the truck bed.

"Well, I ain't never seen such a thing," Dennis's father said with a slight laugh.

"You ain't seen nothing," Dennis, Kyle, and I said all at the same time.

"Watch this, Pop," Dennis said softly, getting up on the back of the bumper of the truck.

He leaned into the back and yelled, "Food! Food!"

Butch flipped over on all four legs, as if he were a pancake getting flipped in a skillet.

We all busted out laughing and Butch walked up to the back of the tailgate, tail wagging and sniffing for food.

He was ready to eat.

43

I quickly called home. Mom answered on the first ring, and even though it had been less than three days, it felt like weeks.

"Hey Mom, we're at Dennis's folks' house getting supplies and tools, and paint for Old Lucy."

"Old Lucy?" Mom asked on the other end of the line.

"It's the name of the houseboat. It's a cool place to spend the summer."

"Are you OK, Son? I've been so worried about you. How's Butch doing out there in the swamps?"

"He's good; he has come to like the boats, and they have four other boats besides the houseboat. Yes, Mom, I'm good, Dennis and Kyle are watching every move I make. I'll make sure to call every time we go to a nearby town for supplies. Thanks for letting me come out here, Mom."

"You're welcome, Son. Are you writing your adventures down?"

"Yes, ma'am, every detail in my journal. I brought two journals with me. I'm also teaching myself to type."

"What?"

"Kyle bought me an old typewriter, and an instructional booklet on how to type. It's not so hard, and I enjoy learning. I'm gonna type about two hours a day in the morning."

"That's great; I am so proud of you."

"Thanks, Mom. Where's Dad?"

"Your dad and the girls are down by the pond chasing those crazy cows."

"Mom, I gotta go and check on Butch."

"OK. I love you, Son."

"I love you, Mom. Bye." I hung up and ran to the front porch.

We sat around that porch for hours, the men talking about things that needed to be done to Old Lucy, and me writing in my journal pretending not to listen.

Dennis and Kyle had hooked the flatbed trailer to the back of the truck and tied everything down good.

They made constant trips back and forth to the tool shed in the backyard, double-checking everything needed to repair Old Lucy.

Dennis's father ran a small chain of gas stations around town. His mother was a nurse at the local hospital down the road from their house. Though their house was in town, his mother had a huge chicken yard, almost as big as my mom's back in Eunice.

As far as I knew Dennis was an only child, and I was wishing maybe I could offer his parents a couple of my sisters. At least they could have a couple more children to raise, and a cat, of course—these were thoughts that ran wild within my brain.

Dennis's mother stood there next to me, and without warning grabbed me and pulled me into a motherly hug that made me miss my own mother more than I thought I would.

"Ask Dennis to tell you about the alligators' cove. Some of those gators have been living in that same area where Old Lucy has been parked for almost half a century. Find that, and then you'll find something worth writing about in that journal of yours. Go on now; them boys gots plenty of tall tales," Dennis's Mom said to me, placing an old tin glass with iced pink lemonade in my hand. "I'm gonna get supper ready."

We sat on the porch 'til way after dark, eating dinner, and going back in when it was past midnight.

The next thing I knew we were waking up to the smell of fresh-brewed coffee and a huge home-cooked breakfast.

44

Dennis called his friend Jimmy on the CB radio, and he was there to pick us up within fifteen minutes.

We really didn't need him, but the fishing boat was too small to haul the supplies and the groceries back to Old Lucy.

Jimmy arrived with his friends, and they helped us offload the supplies into Jimmy's airboat and another airboat.

"Hey, who's going to drive this boat?" I asked, as Kyle and Dennis went to get on the airboat with Jimmy. It was a huge boat that sat six people, and it was packed with our supplies. They would have to come back for another round of supplies.

"You and Butch are, so keep track of us, and don't get lost," Kyle said, pulling the cord on the back of the engine, making it roar to life.

"Here," Kyle said, pulling my rifle from under the seat of Dennis's truck. I forgot we had packed it before we left yesterday. "Just in case. You recall where the kill spot is?"

"Yes," I said, putting the Winchester next to the engine. I had Butch sit on the metal floor next to the small metal bench I sat on to drive the boat.

Butch had walked on the small fishing boat without a hassle; then again, he was sitting right next to all the grocery bags, breathing in all the aromas.

He wouldn't tear into any of the bags. He knew better, he was just happy to be next to that much food.

I took a deep breath of the muggy, hot, humid swamp air and felt free.

I pushed the handle on the little motor and kept about fifty to one hundred feet back from the airboats that were flying over the swamps.

The ripples on the water disturbed everything that lurked underneath the surface, and an alligator popped up at the left side of my boat.

I went to open my mouth to scream at the guys, and I realized they were way, way ahead of me.

They had taken a turn in the swamp—right or left, I did not know.

The alligator opened his mouth wide, swimming right for the boat as if he meant to eat us. His front teeth clamped down on the port side of the boat.

Butch backed up near three feet closer to me, barking, and I yelled at the thing there in front of us.

Butch's back rose in the air like a cat, and he started barking like mad.

The gator did not let go. It seemed to be dead set on eating us and everything in the boat.

The gator's weight started dragging the boat hard to port to where water started pouring in over the side, and we slowed to a crawl on the surface.

If I didn't do something quick, he was going to jump right in or pull us under.

I kept the throttle on the motor at midspeed and slung a can of pork-n-beans at him, hard.

It caught him square in the nose but did nothing. The gator just clamped down tighter. I could hear the boat bending in its teeth. The sound of the aluminum frame within the jaws of an alligator was felt in my bones, and it freaked me out.

I yanked out another can of pork-n-beans from the same bag and slung it harder than before and caught it dead in its left eyeball. It immediately let go and vanished under the murky water.

My heart pounded in my chest as we sped off.

I found where Old Lucy was, thanks to the yellow flag at the top of the tree. It wasn't hard to find, and I kept a mental picture of all that had just happened so I could write it all down later.

None of the guys asked where I was.

They wouldn't have believed me anyway; I didn't believe it myself. I kept wondering if my mind hadn't just made it all up to add to the summer adventure.

I was always the one for telling stories, and I wanted to hear the one about a certain gator's darkest secret before I went to sleep for the night.

"Where were you?" Kyle finally asked, grabbing the small generator and hauling it up near the cypress tree to the left side of Old Lucy.

"A gator bit the side of the boat and wouldn't let go. I threw two cans of pork-n-beans at it. The second one caught it dead in the eyeball; it let go, and we took off. Sorry, this boat got some water in it and some of the bags are wet."

That was all that was said. No one said or did anything. There was nothing to be done. This was their land, and we were strangers here.

The next several hours were spent inspecting the damage in the houseboat, cleaning up, and putting the groceries away.

"Hey, what about that snake?" I asked, as we all stood around in the kitchen area eating sandwiches and drinking cold root beers.

"Do you think it might be dead?" Kyle asked.

"I threw it out, back into the water before we even pulled Old Lucy up from the dead," said Dennis.

45

A light fog started to slither around the swampy lagoon. The inside of the houseboat still smelled of dampness, so a few candles were lit and placed throughout the living and sleeping area of Old Lucy.

It took less than a couple hours for us to snap a chalk line completely around the inside of the houseboat. Then all three of us worked at ripping the old beadboard from the base of the floor to the chalk line. We made a pile of trash just behind Old Lucy on the shore.

I left Butch out on the deck in the shade of the front overhang of the rooftop, tied to the right of the door that went inside the houseboat.

Inside, the three of us went over the list of things to do for the next couple of days.

"I want to hear about the alligators' cove," I said.

"I don't have a clue as to what you're talking about," Dennis said, sitting down on the old built-in bench behind the table.

"Oh, come on, your mom told me to ask you. She said it was a story worth writing about."

I hung on the edge of my chair hoping to hear the story.

"It's really late, it's been a long, long day, and I'm not up to telling it tonight."

I was ready for sleep anyhow. Suddenly I heard Butch barking; it was a yelp of pain.

I forgot he was outside, and all three of us ran outside to check on him.

He had chased a huge crawfish around the deck, or as far as the ten-foot chain would allow.

The crawfish had gotten clamped onto his left ear.

Butch kept running around in circles, shaking his head violently.

He was trying hard to shake the crawfish free from his ear.

He let out another yelp of pain.

We had to get that crawfish from Butch's ear!

"Come here, boy! Come here," I called, running up to him, but he wouldn't keep still.

He kept on whining and walking around in circles, shaking his head back and forth violently.

I felt bad for my dog.

I felt his pain, and tears started to come to my eyes, but I refused to let them show.

Dennis put his right hand out and said softly, "Sit." And without a fuss, my dog instantly listened. I was more than a little shocked by that, like Dennis had put Butch under a spell.

Kyle grabbed the crawfish and snapped both its claws from its body and tossed the clawless crawfish into the water.

Kyle had to pry the claws from Butch's ear.

Kyle picked Butch up, and we hauled him inside and laid him on the table.

"It's not that bad," Kyle said, washing some of the blood from the wound with a rag Dennis handed him.

"Hold him down, you guys. He's going to be real jumpy when I apply pressure." Kyle pressed the wet rag firmly against Butch's ear.

"It's OK, boy, it's OK," Kyle said, rubbing Butch on the back of the head. A few more minutes of pressure, and the bleeding stopped, and Butch was back to normal as if it had never happened to begin with.

"I'll bet you'll think twice about messing with another crawfish, won't you, boy," said Kyle. "Where did it come from? is the real question. If there had been a bunch of them on the deck, we'd had a nice dinner," Kyle said with a laugh.

"Amen," said Dennis, and we all laughed. Sleep came fast and easy. I held Butch close to me like a teddy bear.

The morning sun rose faster than it faded last night, and Dennis was already up. He brewed coffee and was cooking breakfast, going over the new lists of things to do for the next couple of days, once again.

He handed me a list of things that had my name on the top of it. There were three other lists, one for Kyle and one for himself, and a fourth list for all of us to do together.

It was by far the hottest morning so far. All I wanted to do was get out there and explore the swamps.

I didn't feel like working to fix up this old houseboat. I had come here to get away from work.

46

We drank our coffee, and then headed outside as Jimmy's airboat drove up. He drove it right up on the shore and parked it next to Dennis's airboat.

The water level at the back of the houseboat was less than a foot deep, for the sides and the front of the houseboat were up on dry land. It was funny seeing the rusted-out metal drums under the deck that kept her afloat.

It only made you wonder why in the world she hadn't sunk sooner.

"I'm here to help you guys repair this boat, so we can get on with the summer."

"Sounds good to me," Dennis said patting his friend on the shoulder.

"Hey. there's another cup of coffee in the pot. It's still fresh."

"That sounds good." Jimmy went inside and came back out with a steaming cup.

I stood there looking at the list in my hand. Butch went wild chasing a huge bullfrog around on the deck. Where it had come from, I had no idea, but I was willing to bet it wouldn't return after being chased from one end of the deck to the other.

I went inside to get a cold glass of milk while all three guys went down into the water and under the deck to look closer at the repairs that needed to be done.

I walked back outside and heard them laughing like a mental nut case.

"What's so funny?" I asked, as I leaned over the deck.

"Nothing, it's just an old college joke," Kyle said, as he pulled himself up on the deck.

All three of them (swamp rats is what they were) sat at the edge of the deck taking their shoes off.

"Oops," Jimmy said. His left shoe slipped from his hand into the muddy water below.

"It won't go far," Dennis said, standing.

I caught sight of Butch in my left eye. He was lying at the end of the deck, with that bullfrog under his paws.

"Hey, you guys come and see what Butch caught."

"What is it, another crawfish?" Dennis said with a slight laugh.

Butch kept licking at the back of the bullfrog's head. It kept twisting and turning, but Butch kept a firm grip on it.

"I can taste it now, some good old fried frog legs," Dennis said, and bent over to grab the bullfrog from Butch.

Butch yanked the bullfrog under his chest and started growling at all of us. It was a low gut-throttle of a growl I had never heard before, and I almost laughed at the sound coming out of him.

"Come on, boy, let me have it," I said, bending over to pull it from under him. He growled at me and bared his teeth, but I knew he wouldn't bite me.

"Give that bullfrog to me!" I demanded and pushed him over on his side. But he held a firm grip on the slippery new toy, and he wasn't letting go.

It was a tug of war between Butch and me, and the poor bullfrog was the rope.

The laughter from the other guys only made me more determined to get the frog from my crazy dog.

Butch had one of the back legs of the bullfrog wedged lightly but firmly in his teeth. I had the front legs slipping through my hands. I was afraid the poor frog would lose more than one leg by the time we were done.

I knew Butch didn't know what it was, and I knew he wasn't going to eat it; at least that was my hope.

"*Food! Food!*" Kyle yelled from behind me. Butch released the rear leg of the bullfrog and ran for his dog dish at the other end of the deck.

The bullfrog started twisting violently in my hands.

"Hold him tight, Champ," said Kyle.

The bullfrog slipped from my hands, hit the deck, then took one big leap over the deck and straight into the swamp.

"*Come back!*" Jimmy yelled after the bullfrog.

It vanished from sight.

"Now there went a perfectly good meal," Dennis said, just before we all broke out into laughter.

"I guess I should go and feed him." I grabbed Butch's bowl and filled it.

"Well, we had better go and get the new drums, so we can fix this pile of junk," Dennis said. The three of them started walking toward Jimmy's airboat.

"Kyle, can you come here for a minute?" I asked as I stood next to Butch.

"Yeah, what's up, Champ?"

"Is it all right if Butch and I go swimming and exploring? We could use the canoe?" I asked hopefully.

"Well, you really can't start painting the place 'til we get it all repaired and floating properly."

"You'll have to ask Dennis about the canoe. These are his boats not mine."

"Yeah, what's up?" Dennis asked.

"Well, I … I."

"You want to go exploring, right?"

"Uh-huh."

"And you want to take one of the boats?"

"Yeah," I said, a big smile creeping over my face.

"I want you to write down every turn you take from here, using your compass. You'd better be back here by nightfall. I've never really named the small motorboat. I guess we could call that one," he said, looking closer at the big bite marks from the gator the other day, "Dent." We both laughed.

"You have to finish your list of things to do if I am ever to tell you about the alligators' cove."

"I want you to take that small alarm clock sitting on the counter in there next to the stove. Watch the time."

Dennis checked to make sure there was enough gas and oil in the engine on the fishing boat. He started it and let it idle there for a bit. He checked the extra five-gallon gas tank, and looked twice to make sure there was an extra quart of oil on board.

"I will and thanks."

"You understand the rules," Kyle said, and they all got on the airboat.

I packed a quick lunch and tossed some cold drinks and the lunch into the small ice chest.

I got the things I needed, including my small backpack with my journal and pencils and ink pens. I grabbed my trusty Winchester and threw everything else in the small duffle bag, with some dog food and Butch's bowls. We took off.

Everywhere I turned, I saw one or two alligators floating near the shores, or under a huge cypress sticking up out in the middle of the swamps. A small black bird flew down. It landed on the edge of one of the gators' noses off to the left of the boat.

I took my hand off the throttle and let the boat drift softly by on the murky water. I wanted to see what would happen next, and in the back of my brain I knew what was going to happen.

The dumb bird walked to the end of the gator's nose. It must have thought it was on a log, even though the nose of the gator started to rise out of the water. I was hanging onto the throttle watching every move that black bird made.

In the blink of an eye, the gator's mouth jerked open; the bird tumbled inside the black hole. The jaws clamped tight. The alligator vanished into the swampy water.

I shoved my hand back on the throttle, and we took off deeper into the swamps. We headed the same direction we'd gone on my first day here, to the swimming area, but for some reason it seemed much farther away.

47

Just up ahead a huge water moccasin slithered across the water. I tried running over it, but it was too fast.

A white owl appeared out of nowhere with a heavy breath of air, and it glided overhead as if it were but a ghost. I watched it glide through the tunnel of trees that seemed to be swallowing my little boat, out here on the bayou that branched off from the swamps.

I had no idea where I was. I failed to write down the directions on the last two turns and that was all it took to get us lost.

The bayou dead-ended into another section of the Atchafalaya Basin. This part of the swamps was different from any other section I had been in so far. There were no huge moss-covered cypress trees jutting up from the water. Just a bunch of rotted tree stumps covered in mold, kind of freaky, weird, and spooky.

I felt that we were deep in the land of the Dead Swamp.

There was not an alligator in sight. I turned the engine off, and all was quiet.

I found myself looking all over the place for that white owl, but it had vanished.

My skin crawled thinking it might have been a ghost. There was no sound anywhere as we drifted farther in.

It was like being in a graveyard.

As far as the eye could see there was nothing but dead tree stumps.

I didn't like this section of the swamps; it gave me the chills.

I yanked on the cord to start the engine, but it didn't start.

48

It wouldn't start at all—just a small spark, and then nothing. I was stuck in a dead swamp.

I kept yanking on the cord, but it wouldn't start, and my heart pounded in my chest.

I opened the lid to the gas tank and found out the tank was empty, which was odd. We hadn't driven that far from Old Lucy.

I switched the gas tank with the hose in it to the full one, yanked the cord several times, and finally it came to life. Turning the boat around, I stopped the boat again, took out my pen and journal, and described all I could see in the journal.

I started the engine again and drove slowly through the rotting swamp. Suddenly the live cypress trees appeared up ahead, and the tree-covered bayou appeared. Up to my right was this huge two-story old wooden shack built half on water and half on land. I hadn't noticed it before and wondered how I could have missed not seeing something that huge. It made no sense.

There were no glass panels in any of the windows. They were all black hollow spots in the house, as well as the huge double doors.

Half of it was covered by trees that hung at a downward slant at the water's edge. A long wooden dock connected to the porch. An old rotting fishing boat was tied up to the edge of the dock just in front of me. Who would have built such a huge house in the middle of nowhere with a view of a dead swamp?

I knew I should have driven right passed it and headed back for Old Lucy. It was like some unseen force that drew me to the dock. There was some current under the murky water I could not see, luring my fishing boat up to the boat docked at this ghostly mansion on the edge of a decaying swamp.

I looked at the alarm clock I had taken from the counter of Old Lucy and found it was ten minutes to five. I still had more than an hour to look around, or at least thirty minutes before I had to head back. I went to turn the engine off and noticed it had puttered down to a slow idle. Just then, I swear, it cut itself off, making my skin crawl. I should have turned around and left.

All was lost in silence. My hands, against their will, tied the boat I was in to the rotting dock. It was so quiet I swear I could hear my own heart pounding. The dock seemed to sway back and forth, as if caught in the middle of a windstorm. (There was no wind at all.)

I looked down and noticed the old fishing boat was more than half under water. Several dead fish floated around the scummy water.

I should have gotten back in the boat and left, but I ignored the words Dennis told me earlier. Me and Butch walked toward the old mansion as if my feet had a mind of their own.

"It's OK, boy, we won't go far. It's OK." Then why was I whispering to myself? I held tight to Butch's leash with my left hand and held my rifle firmly in my right hand. "Leave now!" I heard a whispered cry over my shoulder, and I jerked my head backward to nothing more than a stagnant breeze, and my frightened dog.

My brain was screaming at me to run.

Butch was quiet, walking up beside me. I don't recall taking one step, but I found myself on the old porch suspended above the swampy water. It happened in the snap of a finger. I looked behind me and felt Butch at my leg. We both jumped as that white owl appeared in one of the windows up on the second floor. Its head was pointed in the other direction and freaked me out as it slowly turned completely around and stared down at us with huge black hollow slits for eyes.

An old set of rocking chairs sat at the edge of the long porch. One of them rocked back and forth as if something or someone was sitting in it.

The sound of a door slamming shut from inside sent me and Butch running back to the fishing boat.

In my mind I heard Dennis telling me the folks that lived back here would shoot me dead first and then ask questions.

I tripped, my foot getting caught in one of the rotted boards. I heard footsteps coming up from behind me scratching at the deck, as if someone were dragging a sack or a body.

Butch was barking like mad.

I picked myself up.

We both jumped in the boat. I started the engine and looked back to notice no one there at all other than that white ghost-like owl still sitting in the window with its back to us.

49

I had the engine going full speed. The nose of the boat rose out of the water, and we went skipping across the water, like skipping stones across the pond beyond our farm back in Eunice.

Butch sat there next to me, his tongue hanging out and his ears flapping in the breeze.

I kept looking around to see if I was being followed.

I wasn't, at least that is what I thought, until that white owl came swooping up behind me out of nowhere.

It freaked me out, and I ducked as its talons grazed the top of my head, stealing the ball cap Kyle had given me. My skin crawled as if taken prisoner by one hundred spiders. I shook my head, regained control of the boat, and pushed the throttle back even farther.

"Hey, give that back to me!" I yelled at the top of my lungs.

I was now chasing that owl, and I swore it turned its head completely to its back while flying, to make sure I was following it.

I didn't stop to look at the directions written down.

I kept looking at certain things that stood out along the shoreline and realized just where I was.

There was that old tree that was split down the middle to my right that sprouted toward the sky like a huge Y.

Up to the left, about twenty feet, was an old worn-out fishing shack I had noticed only this morning. Directly in front of the boat were two huge grandfather cypress trees draped in moss. They were two of the largest trees around, and I had to go right through both. It felt like driving through a door to another time and place.

The owl turned sharply to the left and vanished for a moment behind the old fishing shack, then shot out from the other side as if someone had slung it from a slingshot. It still had hold of my hat. It was flying swiftly, silently, as if it weren't there at all, fifteen feet in front of me and barely a foot above the surface of the murky water. Its stealthy shadows soared in the water so clearly, I swore there were two of them, and one was not a shadow at all.

"Please, don't drop my hat!" I shouted over the roar of the engine.

I could see the yellow flag at the top of the cypress that was in the middle of the lagoon where Old Lucy was parked. I turned sharply to the left and gained four feet between the owl and me.

Suddenly, it flapped its wings harder and flew straight up into the sky above the cypress with the yellow flag and dropped my hat practically at the top of that tree.

I rode up to the side of Old Lucy. I turned to look back at the cypress tree and noticed the white owl was nowhere to be seen. It had vanished, like the ghost I was starting to believe it was.

50

"Looks like you had a run in with Scar," Dennis said, standing on the shore looking in my direction.

"What are you talking about?"

"The owl you were chasing who dropped your hat up there at the top of the tree," Dennis said, placing his hand on my shoulder.

"You saw it?" I asked, thinking I was losing my mind.

"Yeah, old Scar has been around for years. I saw him fly up there and drop your hat."

"How do we get it down? I want my hat back," I said.

"It's pretty easy. There are wooden slats nailed in as stairs on the back side of the tree."

"Are you joking?" I asked, watching Butch chasing a small turtle around on the grassy shore, where Old Lucy's repairs were happening.

"No. This has been our lagoon since I was a kid, younger than you," Dennis said, walking over to the airboat.

"Come on. Let's get it before the rain moves in. I wouldn't want to climb a moss- covered tree when it is wet. One slip and that is all she wrote. There would be nothing to write home about, if you get my drift."

"Are you all right if I go and get my hat way up there?" I asked Kyle, pointing my finger up into the sky.

"Be careful. If you fall, I'm going to kill you, and I'll say that an alligator ate you."

I had to look at Kyle twice to be sure if I heard him.

"I'm just joking; go on, but pay attention to Dennis. I'll stay here with Butch."

We jumped on the airboat and drove out to the side of the cypress jutting up out of the swamp.

Sure enough there were old wooden boards nailed to the tree that seemed to disappear into the moss, up to the clouds.

"You first," Dennis said, tossing a homemade anchor overboard.

"Are you crazy?" I asked, looking back at Kyle and Jimmy who were standing back on the shore, watching every move we made.

"It's your hat. You're the one who spooked the owl and gave him your hat."

"I didn't spook that thing. I think it is the devil."

"You could be right. It's been around forever."

"We better get going before the boat starts to drift from the back of the tree. Then we'll have to swim a bit to get back to the ladder, and then you know what will happen?"

"What?"

"Gators," Dennis said, looking up into the sky.

"How deep is the water below the tree?" I asked, reaching out for the slat nailed into the tree.

"Right where we're parked, the water is only about three to four feet deep. If you look down, you can see the bottom. The water in this lagoon is a lot clearer than you'd think."

I peered down into the water, and for the first time paid attention to how clear the water really was.

Dennis cupped his hands, and I stepped into them. He pushed me up, and I grabbed the board tighter and began to climb.

"Watch out for snakes," Dennis said as I hit the tenth board, my head just below the first branch.

"What?" I said, my hands starting to drip with sweat.

"Did you forget you're in the middle of the largest swamp in the United States? Snakes tend to hang out in trees."

"Why did you make me go first then?" I asked, suddenly wishing I was down there.

"In case you slip and fall, I could catch you.

"Keep going; it's a long, long way to the top."

51

I looked down and noticed the boat swaying in the water. Dennis was clinging to the tree under me.

"They're all there, all 159 of them." Dennis waited for me to move on.

"I don't see any more of them."

"You see how the moss sticks out over a bump? The bumps are all slats. Don't remove the moss, or the slats will be covered in slime and mildew, and we shall slip down into the pit of gators."

"Are you trying to freak me out?"

"You're a thirteen-year-old boy living in the swamps for the entire summer. You'll find this to be one wild adventure. Relax a little; ya too young ta be so edgy."

We pushed through tons of moss, up higher and higher into the huge cypress tree. Dennis was right behind me. We both stopped for a moment to catch our breath.

"Ya alright?" Dennis asked.

"Yeah, I'm just looking around."

"Keep going. About fifteen feet higher, there is a little wooden platform."

We climbed through a small opening of moss, and sure enough there was a wooden platform about six feet by six feet in a half circle around the middle of the tree. The yellow flag was right above my head.

My hat was lying at the edge of the platform.

"So, you went into that old ghostly mansion at the edge of the dead swamp?" Dennis asked standing there looking over at Kyle and Jimmy who waved up at us from the shore.

"How did you know?" I asked.

"Because I know that's where Scar lives, and he wouldn't have chased you if you hadn't been trespassing."

"I'm sorry. I know you told me not to go snooping around people's houses. But that ghostly mansion is falling apart. There was no way anyone could live there," I said, watching as Dennis pulled an old pair of binoculars from a branch just below the yellow flag.

"But someone does live there."

"Who?" I asked, as Dennis looked around through the binoculars.

"The ghost of old one-eyed Bobby Ato'Fee."

52

"The ghost of one-eyed Bobby Ato'Fee," I said, trying not to laugh.

"I know it sounds kind of funny. He lost his eye in a knife fight."

"I thought I was full of tall tales," I said looking at all the dark clouds rolling in.

"It's the truth. It happened right over there where Kyle and Jimmy are standing."

As far as the eye could see there were lagoons, and miles and miles of swamp in every direction. I scanned the entire lagoon through the binoculars Dennis handed to me.

A little shack was down there to the left of where we stood up in the tree, and another shack on the far right of where Kyle and Jimmy kept looking up at us. Huge drums were behind each of the shacks. There were what seemed to be three huge pits just beyond the tree line that enclosed most of the lagoon.

An old excavator that had obviously been used to dig the pits was in the pit behind us, and it was tilted dangerously to the left, about to fall over. I knew what the machine was, but how had it gotten way back here in the swamps is what I wanted to know.

"What are those two shacks at both the left and right of the tree we're in?" I asked, pointing beyond the edge of the binoculars.

"They're just storage sheds, for extra supplies for the houseboat and the other two boats."

"What about the freshly dug ditches at either side of the shacks leading away into the woods and those huge pits? And how in the world did that excavator get out here?" I asked.

"That, my boy is an old junky excavator that has been on its last legs for years. My father thought it would be perfect for what needed to happen out here, so he hired a buddy of his to float it out here on a small tugboat in the dead of night. No questions were ever asked. Of course, you'd be surprised what folks will do for a little extra cash. Those are overflow ditches to let the water flow," Dennis said.

"Let the water flow from where?" I asked, scanning the swamps once again with the binoculars.

"From this here lagoon we're going to blow up."

"What are you talking about?" I asked, suddenly feeling dizzy.

I sat down on the edge of the platform, my legs hanging over the edge.

Suddenly—without warning—the platform where I was sitting cracked, and the wood splintered out from under me. I started to tumble down.

53

"*Aaaawww! Help!*" I screamed at the top of my lungs. I slammed into one huge branch six feet below the platform. I hit it with my upper chest. The force knocked me over backward and stole my breath.

"*Help me!*" I cried, hitting another branch.

"*Grab on to something!*" Dennis yelled, climbing backward down the slats as fast as he could.

I knew there was no way he could get to me.

I caught a glimpse out of my right eye on my free fall, and out of nowhere two alligators appeared at the bottom of the tree.

I saw them snapping at air in the crystal-clear water below, waiting for me to plunge into their wide-open mouths.

My shirt got caught on the edge of a branch sticking out of a larger tree limb, which caught me in midair and yanked me to a full-on stop.

The tear in my shirt was getting larger. The ripping of fabric from my shirt against my eardrums, and my pounding heart in my chest were unbelievably loud. The sudden fear of death poured on me like a cold sweat that soaked my entire body.

A branch was within my grasp, so I reached out and tried pulling myself up, but my chest hurt too bad. I let my hands fall back to my sides. The shirt held me for the moment as I looked down at the two alligators. All I could think was where did they come from, and could they climb trees?

Big tears dripped from my eyes, slipping down from my face. My entire body ached. I just hung there like clothes hanging on a line back on our farm.

"*Hang on! Hang on, Sport, I'm almost there.*" I heard Dennis yell above me.

I heard Jimmy's airboat as it roared over to the bottom of the tree, and the gators vanished.

I was still hanging in midair about twenty feet above the water.

Kyle and Butch were standing on the airboat as Jimmy held the boat in place under me.

I turned to see Dennis's feet coming down through the moss over me.

"I hurt so bad!" I moaned, and Dennis came eye to eye with me.

"I'm coming up," Kyle called from below us.

"No, don't come up. I'm not sure the slats will hold all our weight. I've got him; we're coming down," Dennis said to Kyle down in the boat.

"Look at me; I'm gonna get ya down from here."

"OK," I said above a whisper. A new wave of pain ripped through my chest.

54

"Are you OK?" I heard Kyle call up to me.

"I think I'm OK." I found my voice just above a whisper.

"Well, quit hanging around like you were born on that branch," Kyle said.

"I'm coming down," Dennis said above me.

It seemed as if he'd been standing there, balancing himself on a branch. But my vision was blurred ever since slamming into the branch above me during my free fall.

"How ya doing?" he asked, making a funny face at me. He came closer in the snap of a finger, and for a moment I thought for sure he was floating like a ghost. I shook my head in disbelief from all that had happened.

There was a bad taste in my mouth that tasted like copper pennies. I'm sure there was blood. I was extremely light-headed, as if I were still in the midst of a fall, falling toward alligators in what had to be coral blue waters, no crystal-clear waters, or was it clear muddy waters disguising what was really hidden below the surface.

I felt as if my eyes were crossing each other, and suddenly there were two Dennises free floating next to me.

"Please don't make me laugh. I hurt so bad," I sighed.

"Can you move?" Kyle asked from below.

Up until this point I just hung there as if I had grown out of the tree and had been there my entire life. I tried moving my legs. They moved just fine.

"Tough as nails he is," I heard Jimmy say from below.

I looked to the right and saw Butch sitting there in the boat staring up at me. His tongue hung out the side of his mouth as if he were yelling at me. "That's what you get fer climbing a tree like a cat."

"I want you to reach up and wrap your arms around my neck," Dennis said from beside me. He hung there like a chimp, his long legs dangling in midair, almost touching the larger branch below us.

In the snap of a finger he pulled me up and off the branch.

"Hang on to me, and I will get you down."

For the first time I noticed the rope had been pulled from the side of the tree. It was covered in moss, but it was the one thing that Dennis hung on to, and it was how he kept his balance.

"You ready?" I just shook my head. "You'll have plenty to write about now, won't you?" Dennis laughed, and I blacked out as we slid full speed on a mossy, slime-covered rope straight to the bottom of a gator-infested lagoon.

55

"You've been sleeping for two days," Kyle said, as Dennis put breakfast on the table.

"Yeah, you snore pretty heavy during the day," Dennis said. He stood in the doorway.

"Why did I sleep so long?" I asked, as Kyle helped me from the bed, and we walked to the small kitchen area.

"I gave you something to help you rest. Are you sure you're OK? Your nerves were pretty rattled."

"I'm just a little sore," I said.

"I was thinking that maybe we should cut the summer short and bring you back home early," Kyle said, placing a cup of coffee in front of me.

"Why?" I could almost feel tears start to burn my eyes.

"You got hurt out here. It is too dangerous. I should never have brought you here," Kyle said quietly, taking a drink of his coffee.

"Are you mad at me?" I asked not looking up at him.

I couldn't ever recall a time that Kyle was mad at me.

"No, I'm mad at myself. You could have been killed a couple a days ago. Your parents would've never forgiven me. I'm being foolish to keep you out here where you could get killed."

"I could have just as easily been killed back at the farm. I wasn't scared falling out of that tree; well, just a little. If you want the truth, it was kind of exciting. I haven't had such fun in years. Of course, no one will believe a word I say."

"Please, please don't send me back! If I go back, I'll have to do all the farm work. I'll have to put up with my sisters all summer long, and I'll have nothing to write about and nothing to turn in to the teacher."

"I don't want to send you back. I just don't want you to get hurt."

I was glad he wasn't mad at me. Maybe there was still a chance that I could stay here.

"You realize if you write about what happened, your parents will find out."

"I've been climbing trees on the farm my whole life. I'm thirteen, and I climb trees. Sometimes you fall out of them. Please don't send me back. I don't want to go back. Please let me and Butch stay here."

Dennis sat quietly eating his breakfast and drinking his third cup of coffee.

"All right, but you're punished for the next three days. The only thing you will be doing is painting this houseboat inside and out," Kyle said pouring both of us more coffee.

56

Sometime during the night while I was sleeping, the guys had hauled Old Lucy back out into the lagoon. The houseboat was back to the same spot it had been before, just left of the huge cypress tree. I was glad to see no alligators there.

The Queen Ann was tied to the dock as well. The Queen Ann was slightly smaller than Old Lucy. She was the houseboat belonging to Jimmy's family. Jimmy was Dennis's best friend since age four. One of the airboats, the pirogue, and the canoe was tied up there also. But the fishing boat and the bigger airboat were at the other end of the lagoon, near the huge moss-covered cypress on the right side of the lagoon before the waterway.

I walked the deck to the front of the houseboat and saw the guys out at the end of the lagoon.

I could barely hear Butch barking in the distance. I walked to the edge of the dock, jumped in the pirogue, and started paddling. I wanted to see what was going on, and I wanted to be part of it, whatever it was.

"Hey, what's going on? Why's The Queen Ann here? And what are you guys doing with that tree?" I asked.

Butch stood wagging his entire body back and forth. He was glad to see me. "How's my good boy?" I scratched his ears and accepted the kisses he slobbered all over my face.

"We're gonna blow a hole in the ground under her roots," Dennis said.

Kyle looked at me.

"What for?" I asked, wanting to light the fuse.

"To get to the treasure, of course," Jimmy said, lighting a smoke.

"Hey, Ryan, this here is my little sister. She is going to be hanging out here for the summer. She's your age; Skye, say hello to your new summer friend," Dennis said. He looked over at me. "She came over this morning with Jimmy while you were sleeping. Jimmy is more than my best friend; he's also my cousin."

"Hello," Skye said, walking closer to the edge of the pirogue to shake my hand. For some odd reason, I liked her right off. She wasn't like my sisters. They would not think about standing out here in this heat, in the swamps with no shoes on.

"What treasure? There's no treasure." I looked at all of them, to see who was pulling my leg.

"Sure there is," Dennis said, carefully placing a few sticks of dynamite under the base of the tree in a small hole they had dug to the right of the tree. He handled the dynamite with caution, as if he'd done it day in and day out.

"Can I light the fuse?" I asked.

"You wish," Skye laughed. "If they allow a kid to do it, it's gonna be me."

"The two of you and Butch need to head back to the dock, right now," Jimmy said to the both of us.

Neither of us moved.

"It's too early in the summer not to be paying attention to adults," Kyle said as he and Jimmy took a large spool of fuse and started to run it along the edge of the swampy waterway, back up into the lagoon. Kyle kept ahead of Jimmy, as Jimmy made sure the fuse stayed just out of the mud and water.

"I asked that question already," Skye said, as she got in the pirogue and put Butch in. She was a tomboy; that was for sure and strong too. I couldn't believe she could pick Butch up that easily. Of course he wasn't that heavy.

"Don't blow it up 'til we're back at the dock. I want to see when it happens," I said, as Jimmy pushed us out into the water.

Skye picked up a paddle, and we both rowed with ease while I kept a watch out for gators.

"Why didn't we meet the other day at your parents' house; when we went there for supplies?" I asked over the back of her shoulder.

"I've been down in Florida hanging out with all my girl cousins. They OK, but they too prissy and quite boring. I couldn't wait to get here. You did a nice paint job on Old Lucy. I heard you have sisters."

"Thanks, and, yeah, I have sisters—three of them. They have to do all the farm work this summer."

"I bet they must love ya right now," Skye said and laughed into the humid morning air.

"They never do farm work. It's always been me and my dad."

"I know farm work ain't easy."

"You got that right. Hey, Kyle," I called over to my cousin, who was walking and ducking under some of the branches. He made his way farther down the grassy banks, toward the small beach area, where we had pulled Old Lucy ashore to do the repairs.

"What's up?" he inquired from the shore.

"If you blow the tree up, won't it fall across the waterway there?"

"That's the point; we don't want anyone else getting in here to steal the treasure."

"How long have you known about this treasure?" I asked.

"We'll talk about it later. Get back to the dock," Kyle said, as he stopped to untangle the fuse that got caught in one of the bushes.

"That's the end of the fuse," I heard Kyle yell over to Dennis. He drove the airboat up to where Jimmy and Kyle stood. All of them turned to look at us as we stopped rowing.

"Get to the houseboats!" Dennis yelled at us, stabbing his finger in the air toward Old Lucy and the Queen Ann farther out into the lagoon.

They didn't move. They all stared icy holes into us, daring us to defy them.

We started rowing again.

Could this really be happening?

"They say the treasure could be worth several million dollars," Skye said. We tied the pirogue to the dock between the two houseboats.

"What?" I said wanting to hear more.

"Most of it's in the history books, about pirates and crooks hiding gold, silver, jewels, and stolen treasure throughout these swamps and the state of Louisiana. Our great-great-grandfather was a nasty, villainous pirate, and he sank a small ship, not much larger than Old Lucy, in the Atchafalaya Basin."

"And you guys think it's here under that tree? That seems a little hard to believe," I said while hanging on to Butch's leash.

"Jimmy and Dennis have been studying maps forever. They believe part of the original map is buried under the tree, and once the remaining two pieces of the map are pieced together, it will tell us right where the ship is buried."

"Where do they think the ship is buried?" I asked as we made our way to the top of the flat rooftop of Old Lucy. We got Butch up there, and I yanked an old blanket from one of the bunks inside and spread it on the rooftop so Butch wouldn't burn his feet. We both had binoculars in hand, and we scanned the entire area.

"Somewhere in this lagoon, of course," Skye said seriously.

"The fuse is *lit!*" Kyle screamed at the top of his lungs.

We watched as Kyle and Jimmy jumped on the airboat, and rushed here to the floating dock that housed all the boats.

The three of them jumped from the airboat to the dock, raced across the deck, and up to the rooftop where we all stood watching as the lit fuse raced toward its destination.

57

I swung my binoculars back to where the fuse had been lit. I could see the fuse as it glowed red and orange in a bright fizz, racing to the tree at the end of the waterway.

None of us looked at each other. We all moved a little closer to the edge of the rooftop; straining our necks to keep a better eye on the fuse as it raced on toward the dynamite.

"Give me that pair of binoculars," Dennis said, as he reached for the binoculars in Skye's hand.

The fuse was now five feet away, three, two, and then one.

"*There she blows!*" Skye screamed at the top of her lungs.

"*Kaboooooooooooom!*" I shouted. All the dynamite exploded at the same time. The tree lifted out of the muddy banks a good two feet or more. Muddy earth and chunks of wood from the tree went soaring into the sky above and around the tree.

Chunks of mud went flying everywhere, fast and furious, as if it had all been shot from a cannon. Clumps of ground and bits of the tree itself came soaring into the lagoon at and all around us before plunging into the crystal waters like individual bombs.

The sky cleared a little, the tree reappeared, and it seemed for the moment to be suspended in midair. It slowly floated, ghostlike, turning to the left a couple inches, and started to fall.

"*Timber!*" Kyle yelled, with his right hand clamped over my shoulder.

The tree came crashing down, completely blocking our way from leaving the lagoon, and blocking anyone else from trying to get in.

58

"You don't seem to be very excited," I said to Dennis, as he twisted the top off a Coca-Cola.

"Oh, I am, but you guys go on ahead of us. Skye knows more about what is going on than any of us. We've been hard at work since five this morning. We're tired. You two go on. Leave the dog here; we'll keep an eye on him."

I looked at Dennis and couldn't help but think there was something more.

"Let's go!" Skye was already in the small fishing boat, the engine running, and she was pulling away from the dock. I jumped into the front of the boat, and we took off toward the fallen tree.

The tree was lying right across the waterway, the top of the tree on the other grassy embankment, her roots completely out of the ground. The span of the roots had to be at least twenty feet wide. There was a huge crater just to the right, where her roots had been buried before the dynamite uprooted her.

I thought for sure we were going to crash right into the tree—Skye was driving that fast.

"*Hey, stop!*" I screamed at her.

She turned the boat sharply to the right, and the boat took a violent turn on the water.

We hit the banks of the muddy ground just right of the roots sticking up out of the water with such force that my teeth clamped down onto my tongue. I could taste blood, and the boat slammed to a stop just before the pit.

The pit was about six feet deep. I looked back at Skye, who had a wild grin on her face.

The next events happened in both slow and fast motion.

The impact from the sudden, violent halt of the boat had thrown Skye into the air. She seemed to be freakishly suspended in midair for a frozen moment. Then the moment was lost, and she flew right at me, and we both flew swiftly backward. We hit the bottom of the muddy pit, which was now filling with water from the new tear in the ground from the bottom of the boat above us.

"Are you crazy?" I asked, pushing Skye off me.

"Just a little," she laughed, as she spit out some of the mud that had forced its way into her mouth.

Her face and hair were covered in mud as if she had just appeared out of the slimy ground. "The crazy swamp monster," I kidded as I looked closer at her.

"What?" she said, wiping mud from her eyes.

59

This girl moved like a cat, swiftly and accurately. She shoved her hands into the muddy pit walls, shoved her shoes into the sides of the pit, and within a few moves she was at the top of the pit, looking down at me.

I had just moved from the muddy wall because the water seemed to be cascading down my backside as more and more water quickly made its way into the pit.

"Don't move; don't move," Skye whispered. "It is right above yer neck. Keep still or ya gonna freak it out." Her voice seemed to slip down the muddy wall and crawled into my brain. I felt the wisp of a snake against my skin, and its weight was suddenly on my right shoulder.

I could see Skye at the top of the muddy wall looking down on me. I just moved my eyes up and down. I didn't move an inch. I could tell by the calm in her voice she was deadly serious.

I could feel the weight of the snake as its body fell from the muddy wall and plopped against my back.

"Don't say a word, Ryan. I've been coming to these swamps since I was four." She talked very low. I heard every word she said.

The snake was on my back and right shoulder. The snake's dark orange and red head free-floated in air next to my right eye. It was hissing, daring me to make a move.

"Don't move, and don't scream. It will go away. I swear to you, it will go away Just hang on."

Her voice was calm, scared of nothing, which helped push me into a world of calmness I could not believe would have existed at this moment.

The snake's body started to slither over my shoulder. Its head was now next to my chin, I could feel its tongue as it slid in and out of its mouth. Its tongue lightly touched my skin just below my right eyeball. I gently closed my eyes, as it hissed louder. I didn't want it licking my eyeball. Its entire body climbed over my back, over my shoulder, and into the muddy pit fast filling with water.

I opened my eyes and watched as its tail vanished into the water below, and I clawed my way to the top of the pit.

"Are you all right?" Skye asked, as she looked around the pit once more.

"I'm fine. What are you looking for?" I asked, scanning the pit as well, wondering if the snake was going to resurface.

"I don't see any sign of any map sticking out of the mud anywhere. Then again, my brother sometimes fails to get his facts straight. Hey, ya sure ya OK?" she asked again, pushing the boat back into the water, climbing in, and starting the engine.

"Yeah, I just had a five-foot snake crawl across my back, but I'm OK." I turned away from her. I didn't want her to see how badly my hands were shaking. I was both excited and freaked out by what had just happened. I now knew what it was like to have every inch of my skin crawled on.

"I've had that happen to me once when I was eight."

"You're joking."

"No, not at all, in this same area. Lucky Dennis was here, and he told me the same thing I just told you. Snakes are not normally out to hurt you. They only bite you if they are spooked or feel threatened, and I don't believe that one was poisonous. I'll have to look it up in my snake book. Do you know what kind of snake that was?"

Of course she had a snake book. *Why wouldn't she?* I thought to myself.

"I believe that was a red corn snake. I've seen a couple of them back at our farm, but never that close and never one that huge."

"That sounds about right, but I wonder why that type of snake is out here," Skye said.

"I wonder why the guys haven't come here yet," I said.

"Because they knew the treasure isn't here," Skye said, looking back at the pit.

"What?"

"Oh, no, the treasure is here, just not in this spot under the tree. They blew the tree over so no one would get into this lagoon, and they sent us over here so they could get rid of us for a bit so they could discuss what they mean to do."

"So now what?" I asked, as we drove slowly back to the dock.

"We blow up the lagoon!" Skye said excitedly.

60

"Please, don't say anything about the snake. Kyle will send me home for sure," I said, as we drifted up to the dock.

"You got it," she said. She jumped from the boat to the dock.

"Did you find anything?" Kyle asked, as the two of us walked on the deck of Old Lucy. They already had a barbecue going. It smelled so good. I wanted to eat it right off the grill.

"No," I said.

There was an old picnic table aboard the deck of Old Lucy loaded with chips, buns, Cokes, and cookies. Kyle pulled the burgers and the hot dogs off the grill, and everyone gathered around the picnic table.

"I know you're a writer, and this story I'm gonna tell ya is worthy of writing down," Dennis said while looking at me. "Speaking of which, you should go and get your journal and write some of this stuff down."

I ran into the houseboat and grabbed my journal and pen from the edge of my bunk.

"You see, my dear boy, it doesn't matter what you may have read in history books, or the adventure books. The truest are the stories told to you by your parents, and the stories told to them by their parents. At least that is what you want to believe, because they are your parents and your grandparents, and they wouldn't lie to you. It so happens that this crook, one of the most secretive crooks in this area back in the year 1864, was my great-great grandfather."

"Our great-great-grandfather," Skye echoed, shoveling a bit of hot dog in her mouth.

I swallowed a cookie and nearly choked at the words that Dennis spoke.

"What?" I asked, writing down word for word what Dennis was saying.

"How do you think my father happens to run one of the most successful chains of gas stations in Baton Rouge? They were all bought with stolen gold. Some of that gold was sold for cash some fifty years back, but what my father had is nothing compared to what is said to be buried in these swamps. From the research we've done, most of it is smack in the middle of this lagoon. At least it is what I believe to be true." Dennis eyed me closer to make sure I was writing it all down.

61

"Pay attention." Dennis snapped his fingers at me. "The house you went trespassing in ..." he said, looking closer at me.

"I swear I never got beyond the porch! Something spooked me." I looked at Kyle, figuring he would be really mad, but he just smiled.

"It's OK, you would have been crazy not to go," Kyle said, starting on his second burger.

"That house once belonged to our great-great-grandfather," Dennis said, popping the top on a beer.

"Let's get back to the real story," Skye said, starting on a burger. All of us were quiet as Dennis went on.

"It was said to have been one of the worst droughts in that year when this lost ship of gold traveled these very waters. The lagoon was very shallow during that time, and there was no getting the boat back out of the lagoon. Of course, he knew that going in. Old Bobby knew the law was fast closing in. He also knew the size of this swamp front-to-back, and he had to do something quick." Dennis took a breath.

"The next few days completely dried out this lagoon. The ship was leaning over on its side with not a drop of water to keep it afloat. It had run aground. Their crew was down to only four." Dennis stopped for a moment, standing up, stretching, and staring out into the lagoon.

"Is ya writin' all this down?" Dennis asked, starting on his second burger.

I shook my head yeah, waiting for him to get on with the story.

"So, they did exactly what we just did with the tree at the end of the waterway. They dug holes, placed dynamite and gunpowder in carefully marked areas around the ship, and blew a hole in the ground under this lagoon. It was a hole that was slightly larger than the ship. He thought his plan worked, but his ship slipped … The ship just slipped right into the hole. They placed dynamite around the outer edges of the lagoon, blowing the dirt away from the embankments and covering the ship with dirt. They took one of the gators that killed one of the crewmen, killed it, and shoved most of it under mud with its head sticking out of the ground at the edge of the lagoon where the toolshed is. It was a marker, so they'd know where to come back to it later." Dennis stopped talking.

I stopped writing and stood.

"How did the ship get back here? The waterway doesn't look half wide enough to allow a ship through," I said, looking down the lagoon toward the fallen tree blocking the waterway that led to the swamps beyond.

"I suspect that one of the two sides may have not evolved one hundred years ago, so the waterway would have been a lot wider."

"What do you think?" Kyle asked, looking at me.

"I think Dennis tells a better story than I do." I laughed.

"So you think I'm making all of this up?" Dennis asked me, as if I would have the nerve to call him a liar.

"No not at all. I just don't see how we have a chance of getting to it with all the water in this lagoon."

Dennis got up, walked over to me, kneeled, and whispered in my right ear. "I told you earlier; the fun is just beginning."

62

"Come here, Sport," Dennis said, walking across the deck of Old Lucy, to the edge of the dock.

"Go on and take a look," Dennis said pointing toward the very back of the lagoon.

"I don't see anything," I said.

"Are you sure you don't see anything?" Dennis asked.

"Nothing, just a bunch of bushes."

"Look closer," Skye whispered next to me.

"Look closer at what?" I asked, turning to stare at Kyle and Jimmy.

"The fact that you can't see our way out of here, makes it that much harder for others to find their way in here." Dennis knelt next to me. "Point your binoculars at the edge of the water, toward the back of the grass near the toolshed on your right."

It was a good distance from where we stood. The bushes and the trees seemed to float on the water. I noticed that there was no land there.

"There's another way out, right there." I poked my finger at thin air, just beyond the binoculars.

"The old saying is; when one door closes, there is always another one that will swing open wide." Kyle looked through the binoculars I handed him.

"I still don't get how you're going to get rid of the water in the lagoon," I said, rubbing Butch between the ears.

"It's simple, my dear boy. It's just on the other side of the sheds at the end of the lagoon, remember?" Dennis said. Suddenly we were back in the top of the cypress tree before I tumbled out of it, looking down at the massive pits.

"You're telling me that those pits are big enough to take all this water?" I asked. We all walked back to the picnic table.

"There are three huge pits dug at three sides of this lagoon. If I've done the math right, there will be more than enough empty space to take in all the water once they blow the ground on the other sides of the toolsheds." Skye grinned. She was up-to-date on everything. Of course she had been coming here for more than half her life.

"Why not blow it up now?" I asked, writing it down word for word. My teacher was going to faint when she read this story.

"Because, we have to wait," Kyle said while starting on a hot dog.

"Wait for what?" I was getting jumpy.

"Will wait for the thunderstorm that is fixing to blow through this swamp tomorrow night," Jimmy said, lighting a cigarette.

"That, and we still have a lot of work to do, before it can all work easily. I know for a fact that there will be no game wardens or swamp patrollers out here tomorrow. I know their schedules very well. Of course it helps that my uncle is one of the officers that patrols this area." Dennis watched me write it all down.

63

"Now, there is one thing I want the both of you to do first thing in the morning," Dennis said, turning to stare at me and Skye.

"You want us to go and retrieve something?" Skye asked, handing Butch the last of her hot dog.

"Being as you are so up-to-date, and you've been coming here for over half of your life, why don't you spill it with what it is I want you to retrieve. I want you to do it with flair for our writer here though," Dennis said (really enjoying every single moment of it). I think we all were.

I wrote down her every move—the tilt of her head as she looked off in the distant toward the fallen tree, the movement in her legs.

"You want Ryan and me to go back to the house with the white owl?" She stopped for a moment and looked off beyond the tree with her binoculars.

"You see Ryan, Jimmy and my brother have studied maps and the history of this buried ship, or what they believe of it, for fifteen years now." Skye opened a new bottle of Coke.

"Fifteen years, six months, two weeks, two days, and," Dennis looked down at his watch, "ten hours, fifteen minutes, give or take a few seconds."

"You writing all this down?" Kyle asked me.

"Every single word."

"There is an original map," said Skye.

"What?" I asked, not believing any of this. It was becoming better than most of my fictional stories.

"When did you find this out?" I asked Skye.

"I've known about it since yesterday morning, before I left our house in Baton Rouge to come here with Jimmy." Skye tossed her hair back on the breeze for dramatic effect. "My dad told me the story, but he made me promise that I wouldn't tell them until the tree had been blown over to prevent anyone else from getting back in this lagoon."

"So, you knew about it when we went down there to see if there was any chest beneath the tree?" I asked, turning to Kyle.

"We called Dennis's father on the CB when you guys went down there to explore," Kyle said, stuffing chips into his mouth.

What about the snake that crawled over my shoulder. Did you want to know about that? I wanted to shout at the three of them, but I kept my mouth shut.

"OK, it is starting to make a little bit of sense here, but if that is another way out," I said, pointing toward the bushes at the water's edge, "what makes you think that someone else can't get in from the other side?"

"Because there is a huge pit on the other side with no way in or out to the swamps beyond that is also hidden by trees. There is no actual way out until we carefully dynamite the land that will shift all the water from here to there," Kyle said calmly, as if he had planned for this his entire life.

"How long have you known about all of this?" I asked my older cousin.

"Since before Easter," he replied.

"So, you knew about this before asking my parents if I could come here?" I wrote it down word for word. I felt like a reporter.

"Yeah."

"Let's go and get the original map," Skye said, leaning over my shoulder to make sure I was writing it all down.

"The map is back at that house in the dead swamp," I said, while looking down at Butch.

"Not exactly, it's buried under the house," Jimmy said starting on a second hamburger.

"*What!*" Skye's voice rose as she turned to stare at her brother. She was playing her part well, as if she didn't already know such a thing.

"Half that house is built on water," I said turning to look at Kyle.

"I know," he said with a twisted little grin.

"Not when it was built," Skye said to me.

"What?"

"The land in the basin is always shifting, almost daily, and quite a bit during storms or hurricanes. Soon that house will vanish altogether." She scanned the lagoon again with the binoculars.

They were all crazy.

"I told you, Sport," Dennis said, "the fun is just beginning."

64

"If there is no actual other way out of here, then what happens to the boats?" I asked.

I knew Dennis had said something about the placement of the boats, but there was not enough shoreline to anchor both houseboats, two airboats, a floating dock, two small fishing boats, a canoe, and a pirogue.

"All of the boats and the floating dock will be on the bottom of this lagoon once the water gets diverted, except for the smaller boats. We'll tie all the smaller boats up to the trees on land. Once we get the treasure, we'll reblow holes in the levees, letting the water back into the lagoon, floating us back to the surface. We'll take off through the hidden passage there, and this lagoon will be forgotten about for another one hundred years or so. But who cares! We'll be rich beyond belief," Jimmy said, clapping his hands like a child.

"I want you to be really careful tomorrow when you guys are out there going to get that map. That house is old, and who knows what's under the house," Kyle said.

"We're gonna make a fast trip into town first thing in the morning for supplies; all of us. Sport, you can call your parents, but don't mention a word of what we's doin out here, or I'll drive ya back to yer farm in the snap of a finger. Let's go. We've got work to do." Dennis walked to the edge of the deck.

Kyle, Dennis, and Jimmy all headed toward Jimmy's airboat, to the end of the shore next to the fallen tree.

"I know more about that house than the three of them," Skye said, clearing the table.

I helped her, and then we went back outside and sat down in the old rocking chairs at the end of the deck of Old Lucy. I read over all I had written so far.

"So tell me about the house?" I asked, straining my eyes through the binoculars to see Kyle, Dennis, and Jimmy creep around the edges of the moss-covered banks of the lagoon like some bank robbers.

Skye was quietly watching her brother through her binoculars.

They all stopped to inspect one of the trenches that had been dug from the water's edge, all the way to the back of the grassy area near the shrubs.

The plan was to blow a hole large enough and at a slanted angle enough to get the water to move freely enough on its own, from point A to point B. Point A was "The lagoon," point B "The three massive pits." Three gully-like trenches between the two would transport the water. It seemed like an easy enough plan to me. I loved it and hoped it all went according to plan.

The last of the sunlight had vanished more than an hour ago, but the moon was full, and the sky full of stars over the lagoon was something to see.

I lit the small hurricane lamp hanging on a hook on the wall next to the rocking chair I was sitting in. The shadows thrown from the firelight of the lamp were almost instantaneous. It was so cool looking at the stars through the binoculars.

The three guys were still out there double-checking their work, sneaking around the edges of the lagoon like thieves in the night.

"If I were you, I'd get some sleep early. I'll tell ya about the house when we get there. I've been up since the crack of dawn. Meet me at the pirogue at the dead side of the moon. Leave Butch in the houseboat. I don't want him to get hurt," she whispered in my right ear.

Skye walked across the deck and stood there at the helm that unlocked the door to Old Lucy. "Let me tell ya sha," she whispered to herself.

I looked up from my journal over at her, as her southern accent kicked in. I leaned forward to see who she was talking to, but there was no one there but her.

"It's a stupid, ridiculous road." Her voice dropped below a whisper, but I heard her clearly. She shook her head back and forth violently as if she were caught in a washing machine, like she was trying to shake off whatever it was she was seeing. She tossed her head back and laughed into the night. She turned the helm on the door the final click, then she slowly walked inside.

She was deep in sleep in her top bunk by the time I put my journal away.

Butch and I crawled into the bottom bunk. I was fast asleep within minutes.

65

I was jolted awake by a hand clamped over my mouth and a voice whispering in my right ear. "Shhhh, we don't wanna wake anyone."

Skye knelt over the edge of the bed staring at me so close that it made me wonder how long she'd been there. She had a freakish crazed look in her eyes; her hair was all wild and bushy from sleep. "Let's go. Meet me outside at the pirogue in less than five." She snuck outside like a black cat in the night.

"Stay; be good boy," I whispered to Butch. He didn't budge from sleep. He was snoring like everyone else in the room. No one stirred.

I stuffed my pocketknife in my back pocket, grabbed my Winchester standing by the door, and crept out to the deck to meet the wild child standing next to the pirogue.

Skye had a lantern on the front of the pirogue, and a couple of flashlights, water canteen, and compass in her small backpack. She had Dennis's hardhat on her head that had the two small flashlights attached to either side with duct tape. She reached up to either side of her face and switched both flashlights on.

The beams of light stabbed into the darkness before the fog. It was freaky and downright cool. We were off on a wild dead-side-of- the-moon adventure.

It couldn't have been any better than this.

There was an eerie, misty fog drifting over the lagoon, moving slowly like a frightened, slithering snake.

A small bag in the middle of the pirogue was filled with canned goods. We both looked down at it at the same time.

"I heard about your pork-n-bean bashing," Skye laughed. We both laughed as we quietly pushed away from the dock. "This is extra ammunition."

"What if they hear us?" I asked, laying my rifle down and picking up a paddle.

"My father would be so proud. Let's not talk 'til we get away from the houseboats."

"Where are we going?"

"Do you really have to ask?" Those were her last words, and I knew we were headed to the falling-apart house in a dead swamp.

I felt like Huck Finn had seeped into my bones, and a huge part of me was excited beyond belief.

I felt on the verge of something huge, like there was nothing that was going to stop us from getting to the treasure ship below the lagoon.

We paddled silently through the swampy lagoon, the misty fog slicing in front of us as we neared the start of the waterway with the fallen tree that the guys had blown out of the ground with dynamite earlier.

"We need to get out here and haul the pirogue around the back side of the hole."

I looked back to notice that both the houseboats had vanished within the fog.

Skye jumped from the back of the pirogue. "Grab that lantern," she said, grabbing the rear end of the pirogue.

I jumped out, my feet making a splash in the water.

"Shhhhh," Skye said, waiting for me to grab the edge of the pirogue.

"You need to get out of the water quickly—never know what might be lurking in the dark. Alligators are more active at night, at least most of 'em are."

I grabbed the pirogue with my left hand and the kerosene lantern with my right. We walked up the small embankment behind the tree, down the path for about fifteen feet right to the water's edge.

We set the boat in the water quietly, got in, and started down the right side of the waterway that would take us farther into darkness.

"There's no turning back now," I said with a grin on my face.

I've never been so excited to sneak out of bed in the middle of the night in my whole life. I've never had this much fun back on the farm.

66

"Wait a minute.
"Stop!
"Paddle backward."
"What?" I asked.

"Don't ask questions. Just do it," she whispered.

We both paddled backward for about fifteen strokes, to the place where we started near the fallen tree. She pulled three huge rolls of twine from a bag in her pack at the back of the pirogue.

"It's the oldest trick in the book, especially when you are out in the middle of the night, in the swamps, on the dead side of the moon."

She reached over to the edge of the boat and grabbed a small branch hanging from one of the low-lying shrubs and tied a piece of the twine around it. She unraveled quite a bit of the twine and let it float there.

We started paddling again, starting and stopping to let more white twine loose, tying a piece to a branch every now and again.

"Are you sure you know where you're going in this fog?" I asked. I was still amused and amazed by this girl.

"I've been coming to this area for over half my life. I know that old mansion on the rotting side of the swamp better than my own neighborhood. I've got a map of this area drawn on my bedroom wall back home. I knew this moment would come. I figured if we get the map tonight, we can be around to watch what those three swamp rats will be up to all day tomorrow. You're not scared, are you?" Skye asked, yanking more twine out of the spool.

"No." I wasn't either. I was just glad there wasn't a snake or an alligator in sight.

"Good, because I know for a fact we are not the only ones looking for this treasure."

"*What?*" I asked, my voice louder than I had planned.

"Keep your voice down."

I looked up. The fog had pulled back a little, letting the moon shine down.

The dead swamp was already before us. We had gone through two-and-a-half spools of twine.

"Give me the lantern," she said as she laid her oar across her lap. "Did you know," she whispered as she opened the small door on the lantern and blew out the light, "that there is supposedly several hundred million dollars in stolen gold and money and jewels lost and buried throughout the swampy waterways of this state? It's all part of history," she said softly.

Skye looked around as if someone else were there lurking just beyond the fog. "Let's just say, we're not the only ones looking for this particular treasure."

She was silent as we drifted up to the side of the falling-apart dock.

Without warning that ghostlike owl appeared at the end of the walkway and sat on the top of the porch railing staring at us with its glowing eyes. It was a creature of the night, and its ghostlike appearance made me again wonder if it was really there at all.

"Let's go," she said, handing me one of the flashlights from her pack.

"What makes you think someone else hasn't found the map yet?" I asked, as I tied the boat up to the walkway.

"Keep your voice down."

"Why?"

"We don't want to spook old Scar sitting up there," she said, nodding her head toward the white owl. It looked like a gargoyle statue in a graveyard.

"We want him on our side," she whispered, her voice even lower than before.

"Why do we want him on our side?" I asked, stepping up behind her.

"So he can warn us when the others arrive."

"What others?"

"My wicked uncle, who knows we're out here, and his two twisted sons. The older one, Bubba, got a case of the crazies. The younger one, Timmy, he's our age, he's not so bad."

"Do you think they'll try and steal the gold?" I whispered as we approached the front of the porch.

'That's a stupid question," Skye said and laughed.

67

"Are you not worried about the gators in this area?" I asked, looking over the side of the dock into the water skimmed over with the milky fog that seemed to be getting thicker by the second.

"Ain't no gators in the dead swamp. Ain't got nothin' to eat here." Skye laughed, looking behind us at the gathering fog that was sucking up everything in sight.

The moment we moved toward the porch, the moon vanished. The misty fog started to slither over the water, across the pirogue, the broken planks of the walkway and up to the porch at our backs.

The white owl had vanished.

The beams of light from our flashlights pierced the darkness and bounced off falling-apart timbers as we stood on the front porch.

I tried to move out in front of her, but she wouldn't have any of it. She was fearless and seemed to know exactly where she was going.

"How come you know so much about this house?" I asked while pushing the door open. The door creaked loudly, and the sound seemed to slam into my eardrums.

"My great-great-grandfather built this house."

"Was Dennis serious when he said the map was hidden under the house?" I asked. I turned back to look at the pirogue. It wasn't even noticeable through the fog.

The fog was starting to slither over the front porch into the house, like a herd of ghosts gathering for a good old-fashioned haunting.

"Yeah, he was serious, but I know where this map is. Follow me."

There was no furniture except an old table off to the right of the door with one chair. It had one missing leg, seeming to balance itself upright as if someone were standing behind it holding the side with the missing leg. It was downright ridiculous and more than a little creepy.

There were both cobwebs and spiderwebs everywhere you turned to look, and huge banana spiders galore.

We had tons of them back on the farm, but these appeared to be a different breed altogether. They were bigger than any I had ever seen. They looked to be actively watching us standing there looking at them. The brilliant yellow on their bodies almost glowed in the glare of our flashlights.

I found myself silently walking across the room closer to one of the webs. The web had to be more than six feet across. I had to get a closer look at what was going on.

"What are you doing?" I heard Skye ask, but my feet kept moving in the direction of the one huge spider, whose eyes, for some reason, were staring right back at me. It was slightly bigger than my hand.

"Leave it," Skye snapped at me, tugging on my right arm. "What's the matter with you; ain't ya never seen them banana spiders befo?"

"Yeah," was all I could say.

The fog from outside had made its way through the open doorway. It spilled in through the glassless windows, slipping over the windowsills and down the walls, onto the floors.

Looking down at the floor was by far the creepiest thing ever. Our feet and up to the middle parts of our lower legs were lost in fog.

There was an old wooden staircase that went up to the second floor just left of the door.

There was a foul odor of something rotting, or maybe it was the aroma of the dead swamp itself, drifting in with the fog.

Suddenly the loud cracking sound of timber shattered the silence in the house, and Skye crashed through the floorboards screaming, completely vanishing from my sight beneath the fog.

68

I dropped to the floor and looked over the edge with my flashlight pointing down into the hole.

"I see ya OK down there." My flashlight caught sight of her below the fog, and I could hear her breathing heavy.

"Yeah, I'm just fine, thank ya very much. Can you see that staircase over there at the end of this room?" Skye pointed her flashlight behind her.

"There's a door just behind that other staircase in the living room. Walk toward the staircase, hug the wall, and get down here quickly. This whole house is falling apart, and I want to get this map and get out of here."

I did as I was told and hugged the staircase in the living room. I made my way to the back side of the staircase. Sure enough there was a small wooden door that opened to an even smaller staircase, going down into darkness.

I took a few steps into blackness. My flashlight had suddenly gone out, and I tumbled down the stairs. I crashed into the floor under the house hard enough to see little stars dotting the air before me. I shook my head while struggling to sit up.

"Welcome to the dungeon." Skye laughed, pointing the flashlight at me.

"My flashlight died." I searched the floor for a few moments and found it at the edge of the stairs.

"Slap the side of it a few times, really hard," Skye said.

I banged it against the floor, and it came right back on. "Nice," I said.

I stayed there for a moment freaked out and amazed, watching the fog drip over the sides of the hole in the floor above us like some sort of waterfall.

It was like some wacked-out dream you couldn't wake from until it was too late. Was it too late; was there no waking up from whatever this was?

There were huge spiderwebs down in the dungeon almost twice the size of the webs upstairs. The banana spiders were stupid big. Their orange, black, and yellow bodies glowed like coals on a barbeque pit as my flashlight caught them frozen in time like a deer in headlights.

It was wicked.

"Okay, there is another level under this room."

"What?" I shook my head, recalling what we were here for in the first place.

However, my eyes were glued to that huge banana spider that was walking sideways like a crab, all eight of its legs moving at the same time. It moved on slowly toward the edge of the web—all while watching me with its eight eyeballs. I couldn't move. The spider stopped, swiveled slowly in its golden-spun web, with those eyeballs holding me in its spell.

"Snap out of it," Skye hissed at me. I felt the slap of her hand at the back of my head. "We need to get the map."

She turned to stare at the spider for a moment. Suddenly we were both trapped by the silence, the slithering fog, the house, the spider webbings, and all the other banana spiders that suddenly appeared out of nowhere. Had they been there all along?

The one huge banana spider overshadowed all the others. It had to be almost eight inches and bigger than my face. All the other spiders spread out from behind the huge one. Suddenly there were more than a dozen of them. They were not happy we had invaded their space, disturbing their dungeon of darkness with our beams of light.

Skye shook her head back and forth hard to break the spider's spell.

"No, you stupid spiders stay in ya'll's web, and I'll not kill any of ya." Skye spat at the biggest of them all. "Stay back!" She snapped at the spiders while jabbing her fingers in the air before them.

"Let's get the map. It's down under."

"What are you talking about? How could there possibly be anything under this area we're in, other than swamp?"

"It's the other level I'm talking about." Her voice stopped cold as the fog drifted down around us, slowly dropping from our shoulders like a cloud falling into nothing.

It was like being in a nightmare you couldn't wake from, where things got stranger by the second.

I stood there taking it all in. It was like being in one of those dreams where you stood on the edge of the cliff, afraid to move, yet something was dragging your whole body closer to the edge, unseen forces pushing you to jump until you woke yourself up and quickly turned the lights on to scare away the monsters in the dark.

"Enough with these spiders already; leave them alone. We have to hurry. Once all that fog gets down here, we'll never be able to find a thing. There's a door in the floor over this way."

I watched her walk into the falling fog and hurried after her. Our flashlights sent eerie shadows into the misty fog, which was fast sucking up everything in our sight.

"We have to get it quickly."

There was an old leather strap handle in the floor. We both pulled back on it and the trap door in the floor with leather hinges came up. The map was drawn on the bottom of the door.

"We need something to pry the door free," Skye said while looking at the crudely drawn treasure map on the underbelly of the door.

We both stood there, looking around, but there was nothing but fog, and it was downright freaky. We bent over an end of the door and pulled with all our strength, but the thing didn't move.

"Wait, I thought I saw something when I fell down the stairs earlier." I pointed the flashlight toward the back of the room near the foot of the staircase and started to follow the beam of light. "There's an old shovel here," I said.

"Bring it, hurry," Skye's voice was slow, thick, and seemed to be stuck in her throat.

"Hold the flashlight," I said. I gave her my flashlight. I shoved the metal blade of the shovel between the two leather straps and pressed all my weight against it. The leather hinges snapped and freed the trap door from the floor.

We both dropped to the floor, gazing down into the darkness that hadn't yet been swallowed by fog.

From the bottom of the house to the surface of the water was only about two feet. I reached down into the hole as the wood started to sink.

"You got it?" Skye asked, as the entire house shook from some unseen force. It caused the very foundation to shift in the ever-present thickening fog.

"I got it."

"Stay close to me," Skye whispered, as if she were afraid someone might hear us. "I've got the feeling we're not alone in this fog," she whispered in my right ear. We inched our way to the staircase, up the stairs to the top floor, hugging the wall next to the other staircase and out the front door.

As silently as two thieves in a fog-induced night in the middle of a dead swamp could be, we made our way back to the pirogue and quickly paddled away from the sinking dock.

69

We started paddling silently along the banks of the dead swamp before we reached the small bayou. Then we headed back through the swamps following the twine. We took it nice and slow. Neither of us spoke a word.

We got out of the pirogue at the edge of the waterway at the fallen, bald cypress tree. We picked up our ends of the pirogue and placed it back into the waterway that went into our lagoon area.

"Why did you think we weren't alone back there?" I asked. We paddled quietly to the dock where the houseboats were, but they still seemed so far away.

"It was something in the air. Something that crawled under my skin. It was just a feeling, and it had nothing to do with all the spiders. I just know the relatives we can't stand want this treasure as bad as we do," she said.

Skye shook her head back and forth violently like a person having an epileptic fit. "*Get it offfffff!*" She screeched at me as she tore at her hair.

"What, what is it?" I begged, trying to see what had spooked this girl that was afraid of almost nothing.

"There's a spider in my hair." She tried to stay calm, but it had gone beyond calm. "I felt its legs crawl over my forehead. Get it off me, get it off!" She cried, throwing her hands in the air and shaking with fear.

"Be still," I said calmly, moving closer to her in the pirogue. Her hair glowed red in the pale-yellow beam of the flashlight.

The hardhat she'd been wearing with the flashlights attached to the sides had been thrown in the water during her struggle against the spider. It was floating upside down, just out of reach.

"You must be still. I'm gonna have to move your hair around so I can search for it."

"Okay." She lowered her voice and became calmer. I moved some of her hair back from her face. She had a lot of hair, more hair than my three sisters put together. "Did ya find it?" she cried. "It's there! I saw it!"

"Not yet; wait, there it is." It was lying against the top of her forehead under a mass of hair.

"Is it dead? Get it off me, please, please!"

"It's dead. I'm working on it. Just keep your eyes closed until I remove its body."

I didn't want to tell her I saw it twitching, and it was for sure looking at me. Those beady red eyeballs glowed in the glare of my flashlight.

I didn't want to mention how big it was. It had to be close to six inches wide with the leg span. Some of its legs vanished in her hair.

I heard it silently hissing at me, as if we were the cause for its death. We should have stayed away from its home in the dead swamp. I pulled more of Skye's hair back to expose the huge banana spider. I grabbed two of its back legs and yanked it from her hair. Suddenly it screamed back to life. It wasn't dead at all!

Skye started screaming as if I had just plunged a knife into her forehead.

The spider yanked itself back from my grip, tearing two legs from its own body. Then it torpedoed itself right between my eyes.

I started screaming like my little sister, Tammy. I was moving back and forth in a demonic dance, staying seated in the itty-bitty pirogue. I was trying not to throw us both in the water.

I could clearly see a set of glowing red eyes out in the water, swimming silently toward us. It had to be attached to a huge alligator.

The spider crawled down the bridge of my nose, its hairy black and yellow legs crawling over my lips, daring me to scream any further.

In the snap of a finger, Skye slammed her right hand into my face, smashing the giant banana spider into my skin. Its body broke open, and spider fluid leaked into my lips. That was the end of it; it was dead for sure. I spit a couple of its legs from my mouth.

We both started laughing like a couple of lunatics.

"Why didn't they try to take it from us?" I asked.

"What?" she asked.

"You said you think your uncle and your cousins were waiting to take this map," I said. We tied the pirogue to the dock and grabbed our halves of the door with the map drawn on it.

"Oh, I'm sure they plan on doing just that; they're just waiting for the right time."

We stood there on the dock looking at one another.

I watched her as she drifted across the dock like a ghost.

There was still fog in the lagoon, but at the moment, it was nowhere near as thick as it was back in that decayed swamp. No sign of any gators, so that was good.

I knelt over the deck, cupped some of the lagoon water in my hands and washed the dead spider bits from my face. My nose hurt from where Skye had slammed her open palm into my face.

I jumped to my feet and kept my eyes lowered to the deck. I didn't want to look at what was standing there at the shoreline looking at me.

I was a good couple hundred yards away, and the fog had vanished from this part of the lagoon. What I saw as I was standing up sent chills racing down my spine.

It was that same set of red glowing eyes that I saw a week ago, in a wolf-like head, standing on a body that was a good six feet tall.

"It's not there," I whispered to myself as I stood at the helm of the door. I knew my imagination was just in overdrive from what all had just happened.

I went into Old Lucy, laid my section of the map quietly on the small table next to Skye's section, and crawled into my bunk. I wrapped my arms around my dog, pulled him tight to my chest, and fell into a troubled sleep while he licked my forehead. I felt his tongue up in my nostrils and sliding across my eyelids.

70

It seemed as if I had just fallen asleep when I smelled bacon frying and heard voices in the kitchen area.

Butch was up and licking me in the face again. I yawned, stood up, stretched, and walked to the kitchen.

"Nice job," Dennis said, looking at the two pieces of the map that had been set side by side on the floor near the door. Breakfast had been cooked, and everyone was sitting around the table eating and drinking coffee.

"You guys can do the dishes and clean up. There are a couple more feet of digging in the trenches before we blow things up this evening."

"Why don't the two of you sleep some more, get up around noon," Kyle said. He started redrawing the crude map onto a sheet of paper, carefully looking at each mark before writing it down.

"You don't have to tell me twice," Skye said, got up and stumbled to the back room and crawled into the bottom bunk opposite mine.

I climbed into my bunk, and Butch climbed in behind me, walking around in circles a few times before plopping down at the base of my back.

It was going on two in the afternoon by the time we woke up again. We ate and then stumbled out onto the deck of Old Lucy.

"Where do you think they are?" I wondered aloud as the two of us took two of the old rockers at the edge of the houseboat.

"They probably went off in search of the other piece of the map," Skye said. She rose to her feet. "It's hot like the Dickens out here." She walked to the dock and climbed aboard her brother's airboat.

"What are you talking about?" I asked, while jumping on the boat next to her. They must have taken Butch with them; he was nowhere in sight.

"You didn't think it would be that simple, did you?" She started the engine, and we roared around the lagoon in full circles, around the huge moss-covered bald cypress tree at the left of the lagoon, sending huge ripples of waves over the embankments. She dropped the speed, and we drifted up to the side of the bald cypress I had fallen out of a few days ago. She threw the anchor over the side and just about jumped from the boat onto one of the moss-covered slats nailed into the tree.

"The last one to the top is a rotten egg," she said, a pair of binoculars dangling from her backside.

She started climbing fast. I wasn't about to lose to Skye! So I jumped on and started climbing up after her, but I knew there was no way of catching her.

"Come here; take a look." She handed me the binoculars and pointed toward the swampy waterway.

"You see that old shed over there at the waterway?"

"Yes."

"It happens to be as old as the mansion in the dead swamp. In it, under the floor, is the other part of the map—or so we've been told. It will tell my brother and Jimmy just where the ship is buried."

I spotted three tiny figures from way up in the tree; I knew it was the three swamps rats.

Then I scanned the trenches alongside the sheds at the edges of the banks of the lagoon. They were deeper than the day before. Small yellow flags were placed throughout each trench, where dynamite would go, no doubt.

"What if there is no rainstorm tonight?" I said aloud.

"I'm sure they will not wait any longer. The longer they wait, the more likely we will have more outside company. Here they come now," Skye said.

Three swamp rats were hauling the small canoe over the path behind the fallen tree and into the waterway that led back here to our lagoon.

"*Get down from that tree!*" Kyle yelled up at us, and they paddled closer.

"Let me show you the fastest way down." Skye grabbed the moss-covered rope at the side of the tree, brought it out about two feet from the center of the tree, looped an edge of the rope over a branch above our heads and took hold.

"Are you crazy?"

"Look straight down. The rope is in a perfect spot; it is a clear shot all the way to the boat. Live a little. How ya ever gonna write such crazy stuff if ya don't actually do it?"

"What if the rope breaks?"

"You chicken." Skye threw her body out from the branch, wrapping her legs and arms around the thick rope. She released her grip to where the rope was in the center of her arms and her legs. Down she went screaming her fool head off!

"Yeeeeeeehaaaaaaaaaa!" She screamed, gaining speed. Within a matter of seconds, she was flying downward. She slowed herself down by closing the gap between her body and the rope. She let go and fell right onto the floor of the airboat that her brother and Jimmy were now on.

"*Get down from that tree, Ryan!*" she screamed up at me.

I leaped out onto the rope, held my breath as my heart slammed into my chest, and let my arms and legs slightly loose as I slid down.

The tree branches flew past me. Skye was right, it was a straight shot down to the center of the boat. My heart was racing like a wildfire. I had forgotten to tighten my grip to slow myself down.

"*Slow down!*" She screamed, but it was way too late. The slime under the moss-covered rope did not allow me to slow down, and I slammed right into Skye, knocking her off her feet and throwing her backward into the water. My vision was blurred, and I blacked out for a moment.

72

I woke up staring at Kyle, Dennis, and Jimmy. "Where's Skye?" I asked.

"A gator got her," Jimmy spat at me.

"*What!*" I choked, jumping to my feet.

"He's lying," she said, laughing from behind me. I turned to stare at her as she stood there soaking wet.

"Are you all right?"

"I got the wind knocked out of me, but I'm OK. You have to learn to slow yourself down, you freak." She smiled at me, and all of us headed back to the floating dock that the houseboats were tied to.

"Did you guys clean up and do the dishes?" Dennis asked.

"No," we both said at the same time.

"We've got to get these boats in place. All the dynamite is set and in place, and we are going to blow things up here soon," said Dennis.

"Why are we doing the dishes?" Skye whined.

"Because it is your job. We have a job, and that is yours," Jimmy said, jumping onto one airboat.

Dennis jumped onto the other, and Kyle jumped into the fishing boat. They were towing both the pirogue and the canoe over to the shore.

"Did you get the other part of the map?" Skye asked.

"Go do the dishes," Dennis snapped.

We both stormed into the kitchen area of Old Lucy, and they drove the boats to the shore. We did the dishes really quickly and cleaned up the kitchen area.

We went back out on the deck, to find the three swamp rats tying all the smaller boats up to the trees at the far end of the grassy land area. They raced back to the dock on the two airboats, climbed up on the dock, and everyone took a rocking chair.

"When are we going to blow things up?" Skye asked all three of them.

"In about ten minutes."

"What about the storm?" I asked. "I thought we were gonna go in the city for supplies and call my parents?"

"No time, and we had all we needed in the other toolshed," Dennis said, rocking in the rocker as if he were a hundred-year-old man weary of the day.

"We're going to create a storm," Kyle said with a cat grin on his face.

"I told you they were all crazy," Skye whispered to me.

73

"The other piece of the map wasn't there, was it?" Skye spoke up.

"You got it, little sister," Dennis said to her. "I want you two to stay here on the deck of Old Lucy." Jimmy, Kyle, and Dennis started walking toward Jimmy's airboat, the faster of the two.

"We want to come," Skye demanded.

"All the dynamite we're fixin' to set off could well kill the both of ya," said Kyle.

"But," Skye stomped her feet.

"Don't push your luck, little sister; it ain't gonna happen. Keep on, and I'll haul you back home in a second. Then you'll really miss out on the real adventure."

I didn't say anything either because I wanted to light all the fuses. I wanted to handle all the dynamite. I stood there quietly watching Butch as he went to his place on the deck and relieved himself.

"I want you and Ryan to get the shovels, the pickaxes, the flash-lights, and all the other supplies out of the storage closet on the back side of the Queen Ann. Place them at the foot of the deck on Old Lucy, and just wait here 'til we get back," Jimmy said and looked off into the distance.

"Don't pout, Skye. You know mom would kill me if she knew half the stuff I've let you get away with out here," Dennis said, jumping onto the airboat.

"OK," Skye whined.

We went to the storage closet at the back of the Queen Ann and started pulling everything out.

"Where are you going?" Skye asked me.

"Up to the roof of the Queen Ann. It's higher than the roof of Old Lucy, and we'll have a good view of what they are doing over there on the shore."

"Come on, boy," I said to Butch while scratching between his ears.

A wooden ladder built into the side of the houseboat went to the roof. The roof was as flat as the deck. I climbed up and sat there as Skye went to the spot where the other binoculars were kept. There were enough binoculars between the two boats for every one of us.

The both of us sat there on the edge of the roof, our legs dangling over the side, staring through the binoculars.

Dennis jumped on his airboat and rode it completely across the lagoon to the other side, where the other shed was.

All the fuses had been set and drawn together at either side of the lagoon.

Dennis ran around with lightning speed, rechecking everything for a third time.

Jimmy stood there waiting to light the fuse that would blow up nine barrels of gunpowder, along with more than a couple dozen sticks of dynamite from the edge of the lagoon.

Kyle was standing on the seat of the airboat that belonged to Jimmy, with a yellow flag held high in the air.

Kyle kept looking at Jimmy and looked completely across the lagoon to where he could see Dennis checking the last fuses.

Skye and I were looking from one side of the lagoon to the other.

Kyle waited for Dennis's thumbs up. Finally after what seemed a longer time than needed, Dennis threw both thumbs into the air. Kyle waved the yellow flag at Jimmy.

Jimmy lit the fuse.

They were all back on the dock within minutes.

I had yanked one of the old blankets from one of the beds in the houseboat, so Butch wouldn't burn his paws on the roof.

"There's no getting out of this lagoon now, kids!" Kyle grabbed a pair of binoculars from the pile of tools. Everyone had a pair of binoculars, and we all stood there scanning the sides of the lagoon, watching the lit fuses race toward dynamite and gunpowder.

"*There she blows!*" Skye screamed at the top of her lungs as the fuses hit the barrels and the dynamite at the same time.

A chain reaction went off on all three sides of us. It was an explosion so powerful, with a massive blazing cloud of smoke that surrounded the lagoon.

It was the wildest thing I had ever seen in my life.

The impact was so loud and so forceful that it shook the ground below the houseboat, which caused a violent shift in the water.

Butch was knocked off balance. He started barking madly as he got to his feet.

Smoke, dirt, and flying debris went soaring into the sky. The midair mud and dirt turned the sky black. Trees were knocked over on both sides of the lagoon.

Within a matter of minutes, water started pouring out of the lagoon, just as Dennis had planned. The houseboats started to sink as the water bled out to the trenches.

74

"How long; 'til we hit dirt?" I asked.

"I'd say an hour or two, as fast as the water is dropping," Dennis said. He scanned all sides of the lagoon with his binoculars.

"Let's go for a swim," Kyle said. He cannonballed over the edge of the rooftop of the Queen Ann, and we all jumped in after him.

The water continued to flow fast and freely out of the lagoon into the pits and other parts of the swamps beyond the blown-up levees.

"Do you figure that our cousins got a hold of the other piece of the map?" Skye asked her brother.

"It's possible; it's their side of the family that started the rumor years ago. We know they are the lazy ones, and they will just sit back and wait 'til we find it. Then they'll try to take it from us," Dennis said. He pulled himself up on the floating dock.

"Do you think the pits are deep enough to take all the water through them to the other side?" Kyle asked. He pulled himself up to the dock.

"I believe they are more than deep enough. You guys need to get out of the water. There's a couple of gators swimming this way," Jimmy said. They climbed up onto the roof of Old Lucy.

We rushed toward the dock and climbed to safety.

"I don't think this lagoon is as deep as I thought it was," Dennis said, scanning the lagoon through the binoculars.

All of us stood there like stone statues watching the water recede.

The boat was getting lower in the lagoon as the water drained out.

Smaller odd-looking trees and shrubs were coming up out of the muddy bottom. That lone cypress tree now stood taller as its roots saw daylight for the first time in years. Its roots were like wicked witch fingers scratching the last of the water's surface.

None of us moved.

It was like we were all under some sort of spell.

The muddy ground of the lagoon came up at us quickly.

"How many do you think there are?" Skye breathed. The scared tone in her voice freaked me out.

I looked over the side of the roof. Swarms of alligators seemed to be everywhere.

Butch was down on the dock, running around barking like crazy at all the giant lizards with teeth.

"Get Butch up here!" I yelled at Kyle.

In a flash, Kyle jumped down to the deck, grabbed Butch, and handed him up to Jimmy.

A gator had made its way onto the dock, and started a full-on sprint to the deck of the houseboat we were all on. It went to bite Kyle at the back of his leg as he was scurrying up the ladder built into the side of the houseboat.

Both Jimmy and Dennis were leaning over, yanking Kyle up to the rooftop.

"There, to the right," I said, noticing an old stick jutting up through the bottom of the lagoon.

"What is that toward the bottom of the pole?" Skye asked.

"Well, what do you think it is?" Jimmy asked.

"Looks like a skeleton in chains wrapped to the pole," she whispered, loud enough for us all to hear.

Suddenly the muddy ground beneath the skeleton gave way and sank farther into the hole. At least a dozen or more gators of all sizes poured up and out, which created a crater in the middle of the lagoon a good fifteen feet wide and more than fifteen feet long.

It was like a bunch of spiders crawling out of a hole in the floor of the outhouse back at my grandparents' house. Gators were crawling every which way, but these were four- to fourteen-foot-long alligators. I was thinking the spiders would have been way better at the moment.

"Is that where the ship is?" I asked.

"What do you think?" Jimmy asked.

"There's got to be at least thirty gators in this area." Kyle said.

My skin started to crawl as an endless number of them came up from the hole.

More and more gators scratched across the deck of the Queen Ann to the dock to the deck of Old Lucy.

"I can't count that high!" Skye whispered, as she climbed onto her brother's back.

"It's the alligators' darkest cove," Dennis whispered into my right ear.

75

We all stood there in the stifling heat. It surely must have been a hundred degrees or more. The heat was steaming from the rooftop of the houseboat.

I had an old blanket for Butch to stand on, which was the most important thing. Oh, yeah, there were the alligators everywhere.

The water kept flowing into the three sides of the lagoon into the large pits, moving like a downhill river. The pits had been dug with an old, small excavator that was now parked at the back of the toolshed on the right side of the lagoon. Dennis's father had hired a small tugboat to haul it out here months before I got here.

All of us—Skye, Kyle, Jimmy, Dennis, me, and my dog Butch—stood there with our mouths hanging open at the number of gators all around us. Quite a few had somehow made their way onto the decks to both of the houseboats and the floating dock.

Their weight alone shoved the houseboats and the dock underwater a couple inches in the snap of a finger, as the water of the lagoon kept receding.

Statue-still we stood, as if we had all been turned to stone by Medusa herself.

We were all hypnotized at the sight of how many gators kept coming up out of the hole where the pole with a skeleton chained to it kept rising.

"Why is the ground around the hole getting larger?" Skye asked.

"It could be some sort of sink hole. Or maybe the bottom of the lagoon has just now shifted from the dynamite blast earlier, before all the water started to move violently to the other sides. Or the hole is just as big as it has been for a hundred years, but the entire surface was somehow, at this moment, maybe disguised as a swarm of alligators. Take yer pick." I was more than a little freaked out.

"It's OK, boy," I whispered, looking down at my dog with tears at the insides of my eyes. I was scared for my dog's life. I bent over and picked him up and held him tight to me.

"I'm sorry for bringing you out here," I whispered to Butch. He quietly licked me in the face. I could feel in my bones how frightened he was, and that alone scared me more than anything, and my heart ached.

This moment made me wish I was at home doing all the farm work, and the house work, and whatever my sisters wanted me to do.

Close to a dozen gators had to be on the deck below us. Their weight and their massive claws dug into Old Lucy, destroying the houseboat. A few of them started scratching at the walls below us.

Like overgrown lizards with razor-sharp teeth, they tried to climb the walls to get at us.

Every boat that had been floating and anchored to the dock now sat on the bottom of the muddy, waterless lagoon. No water was left directly under us at all.

We could easily hear the sound some of the gators made, as their claws scratched at the metal barrels below the decks that held up the houseboats; it was massively amplified by the absence of water.

It was way worse than all the moments my teacher would rake her fingernails down the chalkboard when she was unhappy with the class.

None of us spoke. We were all lost in our own fears of death, of being eaten alive.

The last of the water had receded, and the bottom of the lagoon was left in small puddles from one side of the lagoon to the other.

There were too many alligators to count. They had all turned in our direction, their bulging eyeballs glowing red in the blazing sunlight. They were the guests of honor, and we were their food pantry.

It was suddenly as vivid as most of my worst nightmares.

76

Quite a bit of the land surface around the hole that had the pole with a long-dead pirate, no doubt still chained to the pole, had fallen away.

The hole had grown quite large. It was now slightly larger than the size of the two houseboats and the floating dock, filled with a bunch of killing machines on four legs wanting to eat us.

Within the pit in the middle of this waterless lagoon was another body of water. It was crystal clear, which seemed to have what we were all hoping to be a pirate ship of gold buried at its core.

It was, indeed, truly unbelievable. It was the story of adventure books, and I was smack in the middle of it, wondering how we were going to get out alive.

It was utterly quiet at that moment. All the alligators stopped moving, frozen all around us.

The sudden silence pushed us all into a whole new world of fear. Even Butch was struck by the horror of it all, clinging to me like a scared infant.

As if there couldn't be any more alligators involved with the day, we watched a few more float to the top of the hole. They waited there for a few seconds, then scrambled up and out onto the empty muddy lagoon to join all the others.

The gators had been silent but then shifted from foot to foot. Huge tails swung across decks, slamming into the walls of the houseboat. The rocking chairs went soaring over the sides of the houseboat. The picnic table and the barbecue pit were turned upside down.

Gut-throated growls erupted from all of them at once. It was mind-numbing and unbelievable.

Butch whimpered against my shoulder as I pulled him tighter to me. I wished I had talked to my family before this all happened. I wished I were at home on the farm helping my dad with the farm work.

We had become prisoners with no way of escape.

77

None of us spoke, which made the noise from the alligators on the deck six feet below the rooftop we were all standing on that much more realistic. The noise alone sent shivers through my whole body deep into my bones.

"What are you doing?" Skye asked her brother.

He stepped liquidly slow to the edge of the rooftop as if he were caught in fast-drying cement that was starting to set.

"It'll be OK, little sister." Dennis's voice was heavy, thick, and sounded as if he were under water, trapped someplace beyond his own body.

"You can't do this!" Skye cried as she held on tightly to the back of her brother's farmer-brown overalls by the loose straps that held onto his shoulders.

The long bottoms had been hacked into shorts, the material cut just above the kneecaps. The shoulder straps barely hung onto the old brass buttons on the front. It was what Dennis wore, all the time—no shoes, no t-shirt. Most of his skin had been scorched by the sun.

As I stood there behind him, for the first time, I had noticed a long, skinny, grayish black scar, or it appeared to be a scar at the back of Dennis's right arm.

It looked like someone had held a ridged branding iron to his flesh and burned it into his skin. I am sure it was way more than what it appeared to be.

"You can't do this, Dennis. You'll never make it out alive!" I heard Skye whisper to her brother through her tears. She was terrified of something that no one else on the rooftop knew at this moment.

She held on tightly to his right hand with the scar at the back of the arm. She started to pull him back forcefully with all her strength as her crying shook her entire being.

She held on tighter, dug her feet into the rooftop, and screamed at her brother. "*Don't you do this.*"

He shook her hand free and stepped closer to the edge as if he meant to jump. Throw himself off the rooftop of Old Lucy in some sort of backwoods swamp voodoo ritual like, as if his skinny Cajun white behind would be enough of what the alligators really wanted.

"Of course he's not going down there. The first gator would eat him alive. Tell yer sister ya ain't gonna go down there. Tell her." I found myself screaming, holding Butch tighter in my arms.

"Be silent," Jimmy snapped at everyone. None of us dared move a muscle; even the gators became still for the moment.

We were all transfixed as Dennis released both of the shoulder straps from his coveralls and they fell to the rooftop in a pile. He stood there in boxer shorts, but none of that is what silenced any of us.

We were all horrified at the sight of the flesh growing out of Dennis's backside, or what must have surely been there for years.

The skin on his back between the shoulder blades and all the way to the top of the backs of his knees was charred, shattered black. It was like fine crisp coals in a barbecue pit, as if someone had pushed him into a burning fire and brutally held him down in the flames.

My mouth hung open as I watched in utter horror as Dennis turned to look at Skye.

"Ya gonna get yerself kilt—killed! I won't let ya do this!" Skye pleaded through her tears.

The late hot afternoon sun fell directly over Dennis's backside, and my feet stepped closer to him. I had to get a closer look at what shouldn't have been there.

He was like some undeniable monster out of a polluted nightmare, or a horror story parents told their kids to scare them for reasons unknown.

The closer I looked at the flesh on Dennis's back I realized it wasn't scar tissue at all. It was scales, hard-ridged scales, just like all those alligators wanting to eat us.

I held my dog tighter. I moved closer to the edge and looked down at the deck of Old Lucy, the Queen Ann, and the dock between the two houseboats.

Every single alligator had become like stone statues. None of them moved an inch. All their heads titled upward, their bulging eyes locked on all of us.

They had become like us, trapped by the terrifying situation we were all in, with no realistic possible way of getting out.

Then it struck me like someone had smashed me in the face with a brick. I slowly stepped backward and stared closer at Dennis's back once again.

"Who did this to you?" I spoke to myself, reaching out to touch what had to be hard-ridged alligator skin embedded onto flesh.

The sweat poured down my face, dripping down my forehead, into my eyes, and blurring my vision.

Dennis jerked backward as if I had touched him with a razor blade. "Don't touch me," he hissed at me venomously, like an irritated snake.

I looked over at my older cousin, Kyle, wishing he would do something, say something, make some sort of sense out of it all and explain.

He was lost in fear, which freaked me out. As long as I could recall, he had never been afraid of anything. He was the adult, and I was the kid. He was supposed to look after me. He had promised my parents that he would guard me with his life, especially now that we were surrounded by countless alligators that wanted to eat all of us.

"Kyle." it was the only word to leave my mouth.

Butch whined against my shoulder, and it pushed me closer to fear I've never known before.

78

Jimmy stood next to Kyle, as lost in his own fear as the rest of us.

Dennis turned around and slowly walked the last foot to the edge of the rooftop.

He raised his outstretched arms toward the sky while looking down at the alligators all stupidly looking up at him.

"I'm gonna jump if you jump," Skye cried.

"You will not!" Dennis demanded.

"Momma wouldn't want you to do this. Please don't do it; don't jump, Dennis!" Skye begged her brother as she tried pulling him back from the edge. She had become rightfully hysterical, digging her fingernails into her brother's arm and holding on tighter.

Kyle moved silently behind Skye, placed his hands firmly on her shoulders and pulled her back from the edge.

Jimmy stepped forward and yanked an old steel can of lighter fluid from his back pocket.

"Why are you doing tat?" Skye screamed as Jimmy doused Dennis's backside and his legs with the flammable liquid.

"Because I told him to. It's just a precaution. The smell will hopefully deter the gators if I can't myself." Dennis looked at his baby sister with tears in his eyes.

"If you can't what, stop them from eating you?" I said aloud, looking from Dennis to my older cousin angrily. "You agree with what he's doing?' I asked Kyle. He said nothing, just held on to Skye. "You promised my mom you'd take care of me."

"Don't do it!" Skye pleaded.

"How else do you think we're gonna get the gold?" Dennis asked Skye.

With those words hanging in the air between all of us, Dennis leaped from the rooftop of Old Lucy and landed on the deck below with a thud in the midst of more than a dozen alligators. The gators should have immediately attacked him, but they did nothing of the sort.

I moved to the edge of the rooftop where Dennis stood a moment ago.

Skye had fallen to her hands and knees and crawled to the edge next to me. Tears froze on her face as she looked down at her brother standing in the middle of death—only it wasn't. The gators still hadn't moved an inch from the spots they were all frozen in.

The smell of that many alligators out of water and that close was horrendous. They themselves needed the water.

Kyle and Jimmy moved silently forward.

Dennis jumped like a cat, from the deck to the muddy, waterless lagoon, emptied, but for the army of stone—breathing alligators waiting for him.

Dennis should have been eaten. He should have been torn to shreds, but none of them even attempted to bite him.

As I stood there looking down, I recalled a legend in a story I had read once about an alligator god or a gator creature within a Native American culture out of the state of Georgia. Parts of that story stated that the alligator god had made it to parts of Louisiana. I shook my head back and forth, looking at Dennis amongst all those alligators. There was no way this had anything to do with that, but why were none of them trying to eat him?

All the alligators jumped from the decks of the houseboats and moved alongside all the others on the muddy floor of the lagoon. They all formed a line as if they were going to war. Four-wide they stood, and clear back to the edge of the hole they'd just escaped from, the hole with a pirate ship filled with gold more than a hundred years old.

Dennis turned to look at all the alligators as if they were pets.

They stared right back at him as if they were his children, and he was their father.

He would protect both them and us.

It was so utterly ridiculous. I found myself slamming my eyes shut and reopening them several times to see if I wasn't in the middle of some whacked-out nightmare.

Dennis turned around and started moving slowly, arms outstretched to the sky, and all the alligators started walking, shuffling, marching, stupidly slow behind him.

He did not once look back to see if any one of them had broken from the spell they seemed to be under.

Dennis marched on toward the very end of the lagoon, and every single alligator methodically marched on behind him.

They were starving for water, despite the fact there was still a crystal-clear body of water in the middle of the empty lagoon that supposedly held an old pirate ship of gold deeper down underground. It was no longer what they needed.

None of us on the rooftop moved a muscle. We all watched silently, afraid that if we moved it might disturb the alligators, and they might turn and come back to eat us.

Dennis walked upon the shore, across the grassy area, and on up to the top of the new levees at the very end of the land near the toolshed.

Land that had been blown with dynamite and gunpowder created the almost ninety-degree rip in the earth. The slanted landslide would allow all the water to freely flow into the massively large pits.

Dennis stood there at the top of the levee, his back to the army of alligators. His hands pointed at the sky and the fast-fading sun.

Every single gator marched on straight at his backside.

"Oh my God, they gonna eat him," Skye cried next to me.

I didn't say a word because those were my thoughts exactly.

Dennis stabbed his hands toward the sky, and the gators split down the middle in formation. They marched on right beside him within inches from his legs and crept on to the top of the levee.

The alligators were indeed under his spell. There was absolutely no other explanation for him to have not been devoured. They did not stop two-by-two; they vanished over the top of the levee. You could hear their bodies splashing in the water on the other side.

Dennis lowered his hands to his sides as the last four gators dove over the side. He fell to his knees in the mud and hung his head for a moment.

I searched the entire lagoon with my binoculars. There was not another alligator in sight.

Dennis got to his feet and started marching to the middle of the lagoon where the hole with crystal-clear water was (with a supposed sunken pirate ship of gold at its core).

The rest of us were suddenly released from the spell that had kept us frozen to the edge of Old Lucy.

We all got down from the houseboat and cautiously crept out to the middle of the lagoon. We stood there next to Dennis, who looked like he'd just been run over by a pack of gators. Indeed that is what just happened.

None of us turned to look down into the crystal waters. We were all still in shock at what had happened.

Butch looked at me before licking my face. He jumped down from my arms and trotted over to where Dennis stood, about six feet from all of us.

My eyes caught sight of a gold coin glistening in the mud near my right foot, but I kept my mouth shut.

Dennis picked Butch up and rubbed him between the ears. Butch sniffed him cautiously, as if it were the first time he'd ever met Dennis, then lavished his face with kisses.

Wow, I thought to myself, *Dennis really was Lord of the Swamp*.

To

be

continued …

ABOUT THE AUTHOR

Calvin Ray Davis grew up in South Louisiana where bayous and swamps were his back yard. Alligators, venomous snakes, and spiders galore crept across every path of adventure. Mystical Cajun folklore creatures (like the Rougarou) and centuries-old hidden gold stories were told around campfires. He has been an artist since the age of ten and has written for more than forty years, has had three self-published novels, is a spoken word artist and a published poet. He was a *Colorado Voices* columnist winner and was a contributing writer for *Firestarter.* He is currently working on the fifth and final installment in this series that was handwritten before the age of cell phones.

Printed in the USA
CPSIA information can be obtained
at www.ICGtesting.com
LVHW090811011123
762636LV00005B/240